# All he could focus on was the way her mouth crinkled...

Arjun had been with a fair number of women in the last several years; all of them had been socialites who clearly understood that he wasn't looking for an emotional attachment. His relationships were always physical. None of them had made him want to connect emotionally.

"Am I really more amusing than the comedian?" Rani turned to him, grinning.

He smiled sheepishly. "You certainly are more beautiful."

Her eyes widened and her mouth opened slightly. He took a breath to keep from leaning over and kissing her irresistible lips. As if reading his mind, she suddenly snapped her head back toward the stage. He took a long drag from his glass of whiskey.

*So what if we work together?* If she was attracted to him, too, what was wrong with a brief affair?

*After all, what happens in Vegas can stay in Vegas.*

\* \* \*

*Marriage by Arrangement* by Sophia Singh Sasson is part of the Nights at the Mahal series.

Dear Reader,

This story is very personal to me for many reasons. The characters are from my home country of India and they struggle with something that is familiar to me: how to reconcile traditional cultural values with modern beliefs. Rani, my heroine, was raised in America by traditional Indian parents. She was taught that marriage is forever but found herself needing to divorce her husband. Her struggle to trust in love is the heart of this story. Arjun is the eldest son of a dynastic family. How can he love someone who is wrong for his family? This is a story about understanding your true self, and I hope it gives you joy and romance and reminds you to be courageous for love.

Through this book, I am sharing some of my Indian heritage with you and a love story that will resonate with people of all cultures.

To get free book extras, fun music playlists and recipes from the foods in this book, visit my website at sophiasasson.com. I love hearing from readers, so please find me on Twitter (@sophiasasson) or Facebook (sophiasassonauthor) or email me at Readers@SophiaSasson.com

I would also appreciate your honest review of this book. I will read your reviews and strive to be a better author with your feedback.

Enjoy, and thank you for reading.

*Sophia*

# SOPHIA SINGH SASSON

---

# MARRIAGE BY ARRANGEMENT

HARLEQUIN

DESIRE

# HARLEQUIN®
# DESIRE™

Recycling programs for this product may not exist in your area.

ISBN-13: 978-1-335-20929-0

Marriage by Arrangement

Copyright © 2020 by Sophia Singh Sasson

This edition published by arrangement with Harlequin Books S.A.

For questions and comments about the quality of this book, please contact us at CustomerService@Harlequin.com.

Harlequin Enterprises ULC
22 Adelaide St. West, 40th Floor
Toronto, Ontario M5H 4E3, Canada
www.Harlequin.com

**Sophia Singh Sasson** puts her childhood habit of daydreaming to good use by writing stories she hopes will give you hope, make you laugh, cry and possibly snort tea from your nose. She was born in Mumbai, India, and has lived in India and Canada. Currently she calls the madness of Washington, DC, home. She's the author of the Welcome to Bellhaven and State of the Union series. She loves to read, travel to exotic locations in the name of research, bake fancy cakes, explore water sports and watch Bollywood movies. Hearing from readers makes her day. Contact her through sophiasasson.com.

### Books by Sophia Singh Sasson

### Harlequin Desire

#### *Nights at the Mahal*

*Marriage by Arrangement*

### Harlequin Heartwarming

#### *State of the Union*

*The Senator's Daughter*
*Mending the Doctor's Heart*

#### *Welcome to Bellhaven*

*First Comes Marriage*

Visit her Author Profile page at Harlequin.com, or sophiasasson.com, for more titles.

You can also find Sophia on Facebook, along with other Harlequin Desire authors, at Facebook.com/harlequindesireauthors!

To all the women who've been hurt in love.
Second chances do exist. Trust me.

And to my husband,
who gave me a second chance
and is my happily-ever-after.

## Acknowledgments

This book, and the entire Nights at the Mahal series,
would not have happened without my awesome
editor Charles Griemsman, and my agent
extraordinaire Barbara Rosenberg.
Thank you for believing in me.

Great appreciation to my long-time
critique partner Jayne Evans.
She is never afraid to tell me when it's
time to hit the delete button.

Most of all, thank you to my readers.
Your reviews, emails, tweets and letters
keep me writing.

# One

*1>He owns the room, even when it doesn't belong to him.*

The first bullet point of the memo Rani Gupta had written for her boss was right on target. Everyone around the polished mahogany table stood as Arjun Singh walked through the door. He was tall, confident, impeccably dressed in a tailor-made suit with shampoo-commercial hair and a take-charge stride. *India's hottest hottie.* That's what the South Asian media called him. The title was normally reserved for rising Bollywood stars or sizzling new male models. It was India's version of the most eligible bachelor. For the first time in twenty years, the coveted title had gone to a businessman. Hotelier Arjun Singh, hopefully RKS Architecture's new client.

"Let me do the talking," Rani's boss, Delia Dietz, leaned over and whispered to her.

*Like hell!* Rani clenched her jaw but resisted the urge to argue. Her promotion paperwork was on Delia's desk. *The promotion that should have been mine two years ago.* It was best to seethe internally; she didn't want to give Delia an excuse to turn down her promotion. Again.

Arjun Singh greeted the bigwigs at the table. His voice was rich and deep with an Indian-tinged British accent that came from being educated in an English boarding school. She tried not to swoon at the way he enunciated each word and rarely used contractions. He gestured for everyone to sit. Rani sank into the buttery leather chair and took a sip of the coffee that an assistant had placed there just moments ago. *Even the coffee is better up here.* The boardroom of RKS Architecture was designed to impress. Floor-to-ceiling windows glittered with a bird's-eye view of the Vegas strip. Every surface of the room gleamed with the shine of money.

They began the meeting with introductions. Arjun's golden-brown eyes moved quickly around the table but stopped when Rani introduced herself. Delia was talking but Arjun kept his eyes locked on Rani. She stared back at him, mesmerized, grateful that her medium-brown complexion hid the heat rising in her cheeks. His right eyebrow went up ever so slightly and she swallowed, her throat suddenly tight. *Damn.*

He broke eye contact and she let out a breath. *What was that?* If she didn't know better she would've sworn she'd caught his interest, even if just for a second. She shook off the thought. A man like Arjun Singh didn't notice women like her. India's hottest hottie had the most gorgeous women in the world lining up for him. An average-looking, slightly overweight woman like her would never register on his radar. Obviously she was reading too much into his attention. Her experience with men was so limited that she'd only ever been intimate with her ex-husband. What did she know about flirtation?

Delia started with pleasantries. "Namaste, Mr. Singh." Delia's voice had dropped low and she stretched out the word *Namaste* like she was a yoga instructor encouraging her students to find inner peace. Rani fought the urge to roll her eyes and got the feeling Arjun was trying to do the same. Indians used *Namaste* as a respectful greeting of hello or goodbye, not a new age chant.

"It is so nice to have you here all the way from India. My neighbor is from Bangalore and I was just talking to him about taking a trip there, though I understand you are from Rajasthan, which is in the north, of course..."

*Ten, nine, eight...* Rani silently counted down the seconds. She got to five before Arjun Singh raised his hand gesturing for Delia to stop. "With all due respect, my time is limited so let's get started with our business."

*2>Don't try to regale him with stories of India or Indians you know. He finds it patronizing.*

Obviously, her boss hadn't bothered to read her memo.

Delia cleared her throat and pressed a button on the remote. Two wood panels parted to reveal a TV screen. As Delia talked through the PowerPoint slides in a crisp voice, Rani's shoulders dropped. Delia had decided not to go with her ideas for the lobby, casino or guest rooms. Not only was all of Rani's work wasted, the generic Vegas design Delia presented was all wrong for Arjun's hotel. Rani snuck a look at him. Arjun silently drummed his fingers on the table and Rani admired how graceful they were: long, slim and perfectly manicured. She curled her own bitten nails into her hands. *Does he like these uninspired designs?* Then Delia got to the owners condo and Rani was pleased that they had chosen her plans. The condo was unusually large for a typical Vegas hotel. *You probably didn't have any designs you could recycle.*

Delia was barely finished with the presentation when Arjun raised a hand again. "Stop. I do not need to hear any more." Everyone in the room stilled. "With one exception, these are the same rubbish designs that every other firm in Vegas has peddled. Including the one I fired."

*3>He's known for his sharp tongue and ruthless business practices.*

Delia shifted on her feet. Rani would have enjoyed seeing Delia brought down a notch but her own mouth was sour. Was he trashing her idea for the owners condo? He hadn't even seen her full design.

"Mr. Singh, could you elaborate on your concerns?" Delia asked diplomatically.

"The only original part I see is the design for the owners condo. What inspired you to use a *jaali* theme?"

Rani's pulse jumped and she looked pointedly at

Delia, resisting the urge to raise her hand like a school-girl. Her boss ploughed on. "Well, we wanted something as grand as the Taj Mahal and…"

Rani inwardly groaned. Arjun Singh closed his port-folio. "Obviously you have no idea what you are talk-ing about and this meeting was a waste of my time." He pushed his chair back.

"Your requirements stated that you want a design that allows for both an open concept and privacy. As I'm sure you know, the *jaali* model has porous walls to let light and air pass through but still maintain pri-vacy. The pattern can be intricately carved into stone or wood. The design choices are endless, and can provide a unique touch for the hotel." All eyes turned to Rani, and Arjun Singh slowly pulled himself back to the table. His stare was fixed on her and her nerves tingled. *Delia will kill me, but if I'm going to commit career suicide, I might as well go for broke.*

"You said you wanted the owners condo to feel like home, so we took inspiration from the old Indian-style houses." She went on for another five minutes, careful to use "we" instead of "I" to describe her work. Arjun didn't take his eyes off her the entire time.

When she was finished, Delia jumped in. "Rani Gupta works on my team and helped with this portion of the design."

Arjun's eyes flicked to Delia in irritation, giving her a universal *oh please* look.

4>*He is very good at reading people and hates credit-hogging bullshitters.*

This last bullet point wasn't actually on her memo but it should've been.

"Most of your ideas are stale and overused. I want more original thought like the *jaali* design."

Rani's heart stopped in her chest, matching the stunned silence in the room.

"Mr. Singh, I assure you all our ideas are unique. If you didn't like these, we can develop some additional options for you to consider," Delia sputtered.

"This hotel needs to be completed in six months. I do not have time to dawdle with more presentations. What assurance can you give me that your firm can understand my vision for this hotel?"

"Mr. Singh, given the importance of your project to us, we will have our best staff on your contract. In fact, Rani Gupta will lead the project." The soothing compromise was offered by the company CEO, Ian Rabat. He was a small, thin man with square glasses and a goatee. His father had founded the company and was the R in RKS While everyone else referred to each other by first names, it was always Mr. Rabat for him.

"But…" Delia started to say something but a sharp look from Mr. Rabat silenced her.

Rani's pulse raced. *Is this really happening? I'm going to lead a big contract?* Arjun's eyes sought her out and he lifted his chin. *Is he asking me if I'm okay with this? Can't be!* In her experience, wealthy Indian men didn't ask permission, they took what they wanted. Her ex-husband, Navin, immediately sprang to mind.

She met Arjun's gaze and gave him a slight nod, trying to look nonchalant as if she was asked to lead big projects every day. But panic seized her. Could she really handle a client like Arjun Singh?

"I am willing to do a limited contract with your firm for the construction of the owners condo, plus blueprints and a 3D interior design for the lobby that mimics the one Ms. Gupta presented for the owners condo. Further business will depend on how quickly you complete this work, and your ability to impress me with ideas for the rest of the hotel. Send me a cost proposal by the end of the day. As long as it is reasonable, you will have a signed contract by the morning." Arjun stood and left the room without even a goodbye handshake. There were ten seconds of silence, and then everyone spoke at once. Delia stood and went to have a private word with Mr. Rabat.

Rani slipped out and caught up with Arjun at the elevator banks, her heart beating wildly.

"I look forward to working with you, Mr. Singh." She held out her hand and he looked at it for a second before taking it. Her hand felt small enveloped in his firm grip, and a delicious current danced through her body. She was five-foot-four and wearing two-inch heels but had to tilt her head far back to maintain his gaze. She met his eyes and her legs turned to Jell-O.

"Call me Arjun." His lips twitched. "Is it okay if I call you…Rani?" He said her name slowly, like it was a sip of fine wine tantalizing his tongue.

"Um, sure." She tugged on her hand and he let it go but his eyes stayed on her. The man vibrated with sexual charm. *Careful, Rani!*

"How much of the condo design was yours?" he asked.

Rani resisted the urge to look back at the board-room. "All of it."

He smiled. Not the clipped polite smile she'd seen him give when reporters thrust a microphone in his face or the fake one he gave at the meeting. This one was wide, revealing a tiny dimple in his right cheek. Rani's stomach flipped, and then flipped again. She'd looked at hundreds of photos of this man in the course of her research and there wasn't a dimple in any one of them. *Can this man get any hotter?*

"I have been meeting with architectural design firms for months and no one has come close to what I want. You're quite talented, Rani. I cannot wait to see what you come up with for the lobby."

Now it was Rani's turn to smile.

"I already have your lobby designed. I think you're going to like it."

His lips twitched again. The elevator doors dinged open and he stepped through, then turned to face her and smiled. A full-wattage smile with the little dimple. "I think we are going to work really well together." He joined his hands together as the elevator doors closed. "Namaste, Rani," he said in a silky voice that melted her insides.

*Namaste, hottie!* Rani stared as the doors closed. Then the sound of someone clearing their throat caught her attention. She turned to see Delia standing behind her. Her chest deflated.

"Rani, I see you're getting to know Mr. Singh."

"I spent a lot of time researching him. I thought I'd take a minute to get a sense of him in person if we're going to be working together," Rani said cagily. Why did Delia question her every move?

Delia nodded. "I read the client memo you wrote on him. I didn't agree with your assessment, but given how things went, I think you researched him well."

It was the closest Rani would get to an apology but she'd take it. There was no mention of a dimple in the memo. Still buzzing from her encounter with Arjun, Rani put her hands behind her so she wouldn't fidget.

"Congratulations. You're leading this project as far as the client is concerned, but you'll still be reporting to me and I'll be watching your every move."

Rani sighed inwardly. Any failures would be blamed on her and successes would be credited to Delia. But that was a problem for another day. She wasn't going to let Delia bring her down.

"Great. I look forward to working with you," she said with fake enthusiasm. Then it struck her. She finally had a modicum of power over Delia. Mr. Rabat had already announced to the client that she would be leading the project. "Can I assume that my promotion will be made official soon?"

"We'll see." Delia said noncommittally.

But Rani wasn't going to let it go this time. She had worked long hours on the proposal, hadn't reused old ideas like her colleagues, and had won her firm the contract because of it.

"I think leading a contract like this is well beyond the job description for a *junior* architect." Rani crossed her arms.

"I guess you're right," Delia admitted grudgingly.

*Yes! Finally!* Rani couldn't help but grin.

"Rani, this is a big step for you so let me give you some advice." Delia's voice was sharp. "Architecture is a man's field. It takes a lot to succeed as a woman, especially in Vegas. You have the talent to make it to the top but you already have a black mark against you. This project can catapult your career..." She paused and looked meaningfully at Rani. "If you don't get involved with the client."

"Excuse me, Delia..."

Delia rolled her eyes. "Spare me. The way you two were making eyes at each other in the boardroom didn't go unnoticed. I'm simply reminding you that this firm has a very strict morals clause in our employment contracts. We didn't invoke it two years ago but you won't get another chance."

Shame pricked through her body at Delia's not-so-subtle hint about Rani's past at the firm. Her ex-husband had wreaked havoc on her work life. Right after she filed for divorce, her ex had shown up at RKS and blown her relationship with her former boss out of proportion. A good man had gotten fired. What Delia didn't know was that Rani had a lifetime of pain gathered in her heart. Her previous marriage had left her caged in a traditional Indian home, stripped of her freedom and dignity. Her judgment in men had cost her emotionally, financially and professionally. She had no intention of letting a man have any control over her ever again. Especially not an Indian man. Marrying an Indian man meant marrying his family. She'd learned *that* lesson the hard way. She was done with traditional Indian families.

Arjun's project was her ticket out of the career rut she was in. He had already fired the best interior architecture firm in Vegas. If she succeeded where they had failed, people would stop talking about her past mistake and focus on her talent. She could finally pursue her dream of opening her own consulting business.

"Delia, nothing is more important than my career. Arjun Singh will never be more than a client."

She looked back at the elevator doors. Dimple be dammed. This was her big chance to get control over her life and she wasn't going to blow it.

# Two

"So you finally hired a firm?"

"Yes, Ma," Arjun said into the phone. He'd just finished updating his mother on the progress with the hotel. "Their lead architect is Indian so she really understands the look I'm going for." Arjun smiled as he remembered he'd be seeing Rani tonight. RKS was throwing a reception to celebrate the signing of the contract.

"That is excellent. How long until the hotel is completed?"

He was glad his mother hadn't gotten comfortable with video chatting and they were just doing a voice call so he didn't have to hide his eye roll. He knew what was coming next.

"I'm not sure. The designs have not been finalized yet."

"Arjun, do not lie to your mother. You would not

have signed the contract without an end date." Arjun swore under his breath. His mother knew him too well.

"They have six months. With a bonus for doing it in five."

"That is good news. You know, *pandit-ji* told me that there is an auspicious date in March for your wedding to Hema."

Arjun sighed into the phone. "Ma, again the same old thing."

"*Aaare, pandit-ji* believes such an auspicious date won't come for another two years. And look, the timing works out with your hotel. All the stars are aligned."

Of course, the *pandit*, his mother's well-paid priest, had managed to find an opportune date that corresponded to the exact amount of time his mother needed to plan a big fat Indian wedding.

"I don't understand the rush, Ma."

"Rush! Hema and her family have been waiting patiently for you for five years. And now that we are business partners, it's not right to keep delaying. Best to solidify our relationship with Hema's family. Come home in a month for the Diwali holidays and we will do the official engagement."

Arjun rolled his neck to ease the tension out of his shoulders. He was running out of excuses with his parents and with Hema's. It was his dream to expand their empire globally but his family's wealth was tied up in assets. He didn't have the liquid cash to make it happen. Hema's family were close friends and had approached him about a billion-dollar deal that was hard to pass up. The Vegas hotel was the first in a planned chain of high-end luxury hotels around the world. The arranged marriage with Hema had been suggested by his parents as a way to ensure that their business relationship was cemented with a personal one. Arjun had agreed. Hema was a nice woman, well versed in his family traditions, and he'd already had his heart broken. He wasn't going to marry for love, so why not marry someone who was guaranteed to fit in with his family?

"Why can't we just wait until the hotel is finished and do the engagement and wedding all at the same time? I'll be really busy the next few months."

While he intended to marry Hema, a formal engagement took the commitment to the next level and he didn't want to go there. Yet.

"If we do the engagement during the wedding week, it will be one more party that nobody will remember. This way it will be special. I will send the jet. You can fly overnight and be back in two days' time."

"Ma…"

"Come on now, haven't you sown enough of your wild rice, as they say in America?"

Arjun smiled. "The expression is sowing wild oats, Ma."

"Yes, yes, wild oats." She softened her tone. "It would be good for you to come home, *beta*, even for a short trip. Your sisters are giving me daily heartburn. Now Divya is on a new kick saying she wants to get a job in Delhi and live by herself. And then there's Sameer…"

Arjun sighed. There was a constant tension in his household between his very traditional and strict parents and his rebellious brother and three sisters. He talked with his mother for a few more minutes about the brewing problems with his siblings.

Ten seconds after he hung up with her, his phone zinged with the melody of "We Are Family."

It was a text from his sister Divya. Please talk some sense into Mom. I'm an educated, grown woman with life goals. She expects me to sit at home waiting to get married.

Divya had obviously overhead his mother complaining to him about her. Subtlety was not his mother's strong suit. He hated being caught between his parents and his siblings but it was the role he had to play to keep the household peace.

Give me some time, I will figure something out, he texted back.

His sister wasn't easily placated but she agreed to give him time to think of a solution.

The rest of his afternoon was a blur of decisions that needed to be made for the hotel. He welcomed the distraction because they were problems he could actually solve. At five thirty, he asked his chauffeur, Sam, to drive him to RKS Architecture.

He exited the Lexus ES at the precise invitation time and instructed Sam to stay close. He hated corporate receptions and didn't plan to stay long.

When he walked through the doors of the firm, he stopped short. A few weeks ago when he'd first come to hear their pitch, the lobby had been unmemorable and generic. Today, it was transformed. Silk curtains in royal blue and gold hung across temporary walls that created cozy gathering places. Hand-carved wooden settees with rich fabric cushions were set between the curtains. A jeweled chandelier hung over each area, throwing glimmering beams of light that created intimate shadows.

His feet were glued to the floor, taking in the breathtaking scene. It was like the *darbar* of an old Indian palace. It almost looked like a painting that hung in his home of what the house's grand hall looked like back when his great-great-great-grandfather was a king, and used the space as his court.

"Do you like it?"

He turned to see Rani Gupta smiling at him. Her hair was pulled back into a chignon and her dark eyes were lined with black kohl. Her lips had a slight tinge of gloss. He liked that her makeup was minimal; she was a natural beauty.

He nodded, barely able to contain his excitement. "I want this for my lobby."

Rani's smile widened and he tried not to stare. For the past year and a half, every business contact whose palms he'd greased to get his hotel built in record time had set him up with the most stunning women Vegas had to offer. None had caught his eye. But Rani Gupta had captured his attention from the moment he first saw her. Maybe it was the fact that she'd seen his vision for the hotel like no one else. Or maybe it was her big round eyes that sparked with a mixture of intense yearning and dark sadness. She was dressed in a generic black pantsuit with a cream blouse. As boring an outfit as a woman could wear, and yet heat burned deep in his core.

*Speaking of wild oats.* He smacked the thought from his mind. He didn't enter into a relationship unless there was an easy exit strategy. And getting involved with a woman at work violated too many boundaries.

"I was hoping you'd like it. I have some *jaali* walls to show you, as well. I was thinking we could use the same design throughout the hotel to give it a sense of connected flow."

*Rani Gupta, you've managed to do something rare. You've surprised and impressed me.* He had been expecting the usual corporate reception with mediocre wines, bloated executives and bland food.

As if on cue, several of the firm's senior partners showed up. Rani faded into the background as Arjun was introduced around the firm. The CEO, Ian Rabat, spoke with an authority that belied his slim five-foot-six-inch frame and took charge of introducing Arjun to his senior staff. Arjun didn't bother to keep track of the names of the men, who wore almost identical gray or black suits with patterned ties. Arjun vaguely remembered them from the original pitch meeting. Each man was the vice president of one thing or another. "Every significant member of the RKS team is here for you tonight, Mr. Singh," Ian Rabat roared with his arms spread. Arjun nodded as if he were impressed but knew that like him, each of the executives was wondering when they could clock out. They talked about the weather, the traffic and the stock market.

"Tell me, Mr. Singh, why choose Vegas for your first US hotel?" The question came from a rotund man with a jovial smile and thinning hair. Arjun remembered that he was the head of the accounting department.

"Honestly, it was about opportunity. I have been considering expanding to America for years. Then the

Sandaway went up for sale. It was the right size, and I thought remodeling and rebranding it was the fastest way to get into the US market."

"You're an astute businessman. The hotel is well built and in a prime location. With our designs, it truly will be spectacular and attract the kind of high rollers you want," Ian Rabat said grandly. Arjun stifled the urge to roll his eyes. It had taken him more than a year to find the right property, and even longer to find the right design firm. Scratch that, the right architect.

"Why call it the Mahal hotel?" The question came from a gaunt-looking man named Pierce Waters, who headed the legal department.

"*Mahal* in Hindi means *palace*…"

"Ah, like the Taj Mahal," exclaimed Pierce. "I took a trip there six years ago with my wife. Let me tell you…"

Arjun stifled his boredom and let the man talk till he found his chance to excuse himself to go to the bathroom. He would've left the party but he wanted to talk to Rani one more time.

He found her fussing with pillows. "You know you're an interior architect, not a decorator. Surely you have people to do this?"

She turned and smiled. "I think interior architecture and decorating go hand in hand. Especially for a project like this." She held up a pillow and then pointed to the intricate design on the wall. "The pillows are embroidered in the same pattern that'll be carved into the wall. When done right, interior decoration flows from the architecture. What do you think?"

The light from the jeweled chandelier threw a soft glow on her face, and he found himself drawn deep into her eyes. He smiled. *Rani Gupta, you really have my attention now.*

"You've impressed me. I think you have a lot of talent."

"Thank you, Mr. Singh."

*It's Mr. Singh now.* "Rani, I insist you call me Arjun."

Her eyes widened for a fraction of a second before a neutral expression settled over her features. "I prefer we keep things formal. A wise man once said that it's best not to let business get personal."

She'd quoted him.

"I feel a distinct disadvantage. You've researched me, yet I know nothing about you."

He took a step closer, into her personal space, to allow a waiter to pass behind him. Her lips parted slightly, her pink mouth seductively lush. The pillow fell from her hands. A hot thunder raged deep in his core and he was tempted to kiss her senseless.

He stepped back, mentally scolding himself. They'd be working together for months, and he was her client. He didn't want to put her in an awkward position, especially not with her bosses in the same room. He gave himself the same admonition he often lobbed at his brother: *keep it in your pants.*

"Is your phone playing 'We Are Family'?" Rani asked with amusement in her voice. Arjun realized his phone was chirping. He looked at the message; it was from Hema. Your mom is planning a Diwali engagement. Do something, please!! Delay another year++

Annoyance churned through him. Hema wasn't ready to get married any more than he was, but she never expressed her feelings to anyone but him. He was in an awkward situation since Hema's father was a major investor in his hotel. Yet she left it up to him to solve their problem. Just like his sisters did.

"Everything okay?"

Rani's voice pulled his attention back to her. He gave a dismissive wave. "Yes."

"You seem a little upset. Was the message from one of your family members?"

Had he let his emotions show so blatantly? He prided himself on his poker face; it was essential for his business success.

"Do you have brothers or sisters, Rani?"

She nodded. "One brother and one sister."

"Are they younger or older?"

"I'm the eldest."

"That must be a lot of responsibility."

"You know how being the eldest is a lot of pressure in an Indian family. Parents expect you to bring the younger ones to heel when they get out of line, and the siblings want the older one to fight their battles with the parents." She gave a small smile and a knowing gaze that pierced through him. He had the feeling that she knew what he was going through and was inviting him to unburden himself. He could picture it, them sitting down on the pillowed *diwan* and talking to her about the crises brewing in his house. *Have I gone mad?* He did not share information about his family with anyone. Nor had he ever been tempted to.

Rani was still looking at him with her deep dark eyes and he felt a magnetic draw to her.

*Rani is off-limits!*

He straightened his back and changed the subject. "I think you're off to a great start with this project."

"Thank you. We should set up regular meetings so we can finalize the designs and start construction in parallel. We're on a tight timeline, and I hope to work closely with you over the next few weeks so we can meet your deadlines."

*Work closely?* He had enough complications in his life. He didn't need one more. Rani pulled at his heart strings in a way that made him want to get close to her. Not only was he going to be working with her, he wasn't sure he could delay his engagement and marriage to Hema any longer.

"I'm pretty busy so you'll be dealing with my staff from here on out."

# Three

Rani anxiously paced the marble-floored lobby of Arjun's office. *Will he attend the meeting?* It was a question she hadn't been able to get a straight answer to. It had been two weeks since the reception. Since the moment when he'd really come close to her, when she'd felt something she didn't know she could experience: desire. Even now, standing in the cool lobby with its funky wall art and bright white lighting, the thought of him made her warm all over.

What happened at the RKS party? They'd been having a nice conversation but then all of a sudden he'd said goodbye and walked out. The next day, Vanessa Knott had emailed to say she would be Rani's primary contact. While Rani didn't expect Arjun to be involved with every little detail, he seemed to have disappeared.

*What did I do wrong?*

Had he read her mind that night? Seen her studying him? Lusting after him?

She'd slept fitfully the entire week. She was either tossing and turning, thinking about seeing him again, or dreaming of Arjun when she was asleep. *Dreaming* was the wrong word. Fantasizing. She had woken up hot, with an ache that screamed for relief. In all her research, there wasn't a single picture of him shirtless, yet in her dreams he had appeared naked.

*What is wrong with me?* She was acting like a horny teenager. Then she thought back to the advice her mother had given her the night before her wedding. *Sex is something women endure to hold on to their husbands and have children.* Like a good Indian girl, Rani had saved herself for marriage, but she wasn't un-educated. At the time Rani had thought about how traditional and reserved her Indian mother was, and felt sorry for her. But after five years of marital relations with Navin, she realized that her mother's advice had been very sage. It wasn't that the sex had been bad, it just hadn't been good enough to inspire sleepless nights. Navin had always said that she was sexually repressed. She figured that either years of her parents' inhibitions had seeped into her, or the fact that she hadn't lost her virginity in high school like all her friends had retarded her sexual growth.

*So what's happening all of a sudden?*

Whatever was going on with her, she would push it aside. Navin and his traditional Indian family had given her a lifetime of wounds to contend with. She wasn't going to get romantically involved with another Indian man. Ever. And the fact that Arjun was her client made it all the more dangerous. She was so close to achieving her career dreams, she wouldn't risk it for some sexual satisfaction.

"Sorry for the wait. Here you go." A security guard swiped his badge against a panel on the wall and led her into a private elevator. Rani checked her reflection in the stainless steel doors as they closed. She was wearing her standard black suit but had bought a silky pink blouse to wear underneath. She'd gained some weight with the stress of the last few years and the only clothes that fit her were her shapeless shirts. The new shirt was her one splurge to celebrate her new salary. Standing straight, she squared her shoulders. She looked good. Her makeup and hair were perfect, her suit was crisp.

*I'm a professional woman, and I'm going to act like it.*

She was sick of begging for well-deserved promotions at RKS. Arjun's hotel would put her on the map. She hadn't dared dream big, not with her reputation still shadowed by the incident two years ago, but Arjun's hotel would change everything. She'd be the architect who succeeded where the best had failed. There was no other choice but to be totally professional with Arjun.

*No more drooling over his dimple.*

When the elevator stopped, she braced herself. She stepped into a polished foyer that featured an oval table with a giant vase filled with fragrant fresh flowers. The only other furniture was two pairs of stylishly rugged leather chairs. The walls were the palest shade of blue. There was no reception desk, but a screen touch pad invited people to check in. It was minimalist but warm, modern yet comfortable. Rani knew these were rented offices, but she could clearly see Arjun's style show-ing through.

"Good afternoon, Rani. I'm Vanessa Knott."

Rani looked up to see a young woman dressed in an elegant white shift dress with high nude-colored heels. They had talked and emailed several times a day for the past two weeks. She'd pictured someone petite and librarian-like but Vanessa was tall, elegant and looked like she'd just stepped out of a *Sex in the City* episode. Rani didn't want to think about how frumpy she looked in comparison.

*Is Vanessa also Arjun's style?*

Rani shook hands with the other woman. "Come, we are all eagerly awaiting your presentation in the confer-ence room," Vanessa said crisply.

Did the "all" include a certain hottie? Rani's heart thudded hard inside her chest.

Beyond the gleaming waiting room was a more tradi-tional office setup. A maze of cubicles filled the center of the space and offices lined the periphery. The sounds of typing and muted voices filled the air.

They walked into a glass-walled conference room where a dozen people were already seated. It took her less than a second to lock eyes with Arjun. He stood when she entered. She bit her lip and willed strength into her legs as she crossed the room to shake hands with him. He gave her a small smile. "Welcome, Ms. Gupta."

*It's Ms. Gupta now?*

"Please call me Rani," she said, bemused. The grin he shot back told her he'd done that on purpose and it had the desired effect of setting her at ease. Once again he was impeccably dressed in a gray suit and a blue shirt with French cuffs. His staff were a little more casual, in collared shirts without ties; some of the younger men were even in jeans. The women, however, were all fabulously attired in fashionable dresses and suits. She smoothed down her skirt, wishing she had also splurged on a new suit.

The slides she'd emailed Vanessa just an hour ago were already projected on the wall screen. Rani took a breath and launched right into business. She kept her eyes on everyone except Arjun.

"Rani, how will you acquire the custom fabricated items in your designs given the deadlines in the contract?" Vanessa asked the cutting question and Rani noted with some irritation that Arjun gave a small nod and leaned forward. Rani could tell this was going to be a long day.

By the time the meeting ended four hours later, she was exhausted. There were a lot of questions and several suggestions for design changes, mostly from Vanessa. It was a normal part of the process but Rani had no idea what Arjun was thinking the entire time. Had he liked her ideas? He'd sat back and listened, letting his team do the talking, until a decision needed to be made. Then he took full control. She silently added to her growing dossier on him.

5>*He is very good at giving you the illusion that you're in charge.*

One by one, Arjun's staff members left and then she, Arjun and Vanessa were the only ones remaining.

The hum of activity outside the conference room had stopped. The workday had ended.

"That's some really good work, Rani. Keep it up and your firm might just get the contract for the full hotel," Arjun said. Rani beamed, his compliment sliding over her like cool shade on a hot, sunny day.

Vanessa chimed in. "We made some good progress but there's still work to do. It's almost dinnertime. How about we eat together and go over the final list of changes and contract modifications?"

"That's a great idea. It'll be my pleasure to take you guys out. There's an excellent Italian restaurant right around the corner." Rani tried to inject as much sincerity as she could muster into her voice. It was an expected part of the job to take the clients out to dinner. RKS spent a small fortune in buying client loyalty through wining and dining.

"Do you mean Portofino's?" Vanessa asked.

Rani nodded.

"We go there all the time." Vanessa touched Arjun's arm. *Did she just pout?* "How about that Indian place you keep telling me about? We haven't been there yet."

*We? Was there a "we" in Arjun and Vanessa?*

Arjun tapped his smart watch. "Sam, please bring the car around."

He gestured towards the doors. "Let's go, ladies."

The restaurant was not what she would've selected for a client dinner. And judging by the creases on Vanessa's otherwise perfect forehead, she felt the same. It was a small place with five plastic tables and a large counter that seemed to have a bustling carryout business. Several white plastic bags full of takeout containers were sitting on the countertop and at least ten people stood in the cashier's line. The vinyl floor looked like it had years of scuff marks permanently tattooed on it. A waiter waved to them as he dropped water glasses at the only other table that was occupied. Arjun led them to a table in the corner. Vanessa brushed the chair with her hand before sitting down. Rani caught Arjun's eye, and smiled with shared amusement.

The waiter appeared seconds after they'd sat down and beamed at them. "Mr. Singh, eating in today? No carryout? And with lovely ladies?"

"These are my work colleagues, Venkat. Could you please bring us some waters and menus?"

"So the food is good here, then?" Vanessa ventured.

Arjun smiled. "It's the best Indian food in Vegas."

Venkat returned and plopped down menus and overflowing glasses of water that splashed as he set them down.

"Why don't you order for us, Arjun, since you know what's good," Vanessa said. She pronounced it *Aaah-arrjun* with a slightly breathless quality.

Rani cleared her throat. "I prefer to order for myself, thank you."

Arjun's lips twitched and she got the feeling he was trying not to smirk.

Rani took refuge behind the menu, taking some deep breaths. *I can get through this.*

Venkat was hovering, so Arjun called him over and ordered naan, rice, tandoori chicken, fish curry and *daal makhani*. Rani had to admit it was a pretty good order.

"I'll have the lamb *saag*," she started, but Arjun shook his head. He pointed to a picture on the front cover and she sighed. "Delete that, I'll have the chef's *thali*."

"Good choice, madam." Venkat scurried off with their menus.

"What's wrong with the lamb *saag*?" she asked when the waiter was gone. The lamb and spinach dish was one of her favorites.

"They use really substandard lamb and it's not very good. You will like the *thali*, it has the best of everything."

Vanessa had the grace not to smirk, and Rani reminded herself that she needed to focus on business and not on whatever was going on between Arjun and Vanessa. Rani pulled out her notebook and steered the conversation back to their meeting and the design changes they had requested.

Their food arrived, and Rani's mouth watered as Venkat put down a basket with fresh-baked naan. Next he set down the bright red grilled chicken that got its name from the clay tandoori oven it was cooked in, a steaming dish of fish curry, and a pot of lentils. Rani's order was a large round steel *thali* with ten smaller round containers arranged inside that had a sampling of various dishes. The chef's plate.

Arjun and Vanessa's order was served family-style and Arjun went about ladling the food onto each of their plates. Despite the delicious aroma coming from her own plate, Rani couldn't eat. She returned to the notebook. "From the list of design changes, I think we need at least three contract modifications." She started to describe them as Arjun and Vanessa dug into their food.

"Wow, that's spicy!" Vanessa interrupted. Rani

looked up from her notebook to see that her flawless complexion was flushed pink. She was waving her hand in front of her mouth.

Rani picked up the small round container of yogurt on her plate and thrust it forward. "Here, eat the yogurt, don't drink water. Water circulates the spices on your tongue. The yogurt will calm them."

Vanessa grabbed the yogurt and finished it in two unladylike bites, then gulped down the rest of her water glass.

"I think I need to wash my mouth out. Where is the bathroom?"

Arjun's face was totally impassive as he pointed her in the right direction.

As soon as they heard the tapping of Vanessa's heels receding in the distance, Arjun turned to Rani and grinned. Rani sighed internally. *That dimple.*

"You could've warned her, you know." Rani was trying and failing to hide her own smile.

"She is very good at her job, but she hasn't gotten the message that I do not dip my pen in the company ink."

*So he wasn't completely oblivious to Vanessa's flirting.*

"You've never dated anyone you work with?" Rani asked.

He shook his head. "I like my personal relationships to be uncomplicated."

*And I seem to be drawn into complications.*

"It's a good rule. So who do you date?"

He leaned forward. "Why are you so interested in knowing?"

She bit her lip. *Busted.* "I need to know whether I

should furnish the master bedroom for one or for two in the owners condo."

"For two," he said, his lips doing that sexy twitch they did when he was trying not to smirk.

"I see." Her throat was suddenly dry and she took a sip of her water.

"I'm not seeing anyone right now, but I plan to have a family someday."

*Arjun with a family. Two-point-five kids and a dog. Scratch that, no dog. Three kids, two boys that look like him when he frowns and a girl with dimples when she smiles.*

She ripped a piece of the naan from her plate and stuck it in her mouth.

"What about you, Rani? Have you ever dated anyone you worked with?"

Rani nearly choked on the naan. *Shit. Do I lie?* Unfortunately her disastrous relationship with her former boss was well known among the Vegas design and build world. He could easily find out from one of the mouthy contractors or vendors. She could evade but she'd hesitated long enough that he'd know something was up. Better he hear it directly from her, then dig up the unsavory version from someone else.

"I did date someone at RKS. It didn't end well, and I learned my lesson. I won't be dipping my ink in the company well ever again."

"Why was it so bad?" Arjun asked softly.

A lump formed in her throat. She hadn't talked openly about what had happened with anyone except her best friend, Em. "Let's just say that a good architect, and more importantly a good man, lost his job and it wasn't his fault."

"Are you talking about Bob Seagel?"

How had Rani not heard Vanessa come back? She said down, once again fully composed.

"How do you know Bob?" Rani asked.

"Before I started with Arjun, I worked with Gankle Architecture. Bob applied for a job, but there was a rumor going around that he got fired from RKS for sexual harassment. You must be talking about him. It's not often that an architect gets fired around here."

Rani took a breath. She didn't want to have this conversation in front of Arjun but she wasn't going to let one more person continue to think it was Bob's fault. "First of all, Bob didn't get fired. He resigned. And there was no sexual harassment. He was my boss and my friend. We had just started dating when things got blown out of proportion." She wasn't going to get into how she'd been going through a messy divorce and her ex-husband had hired a private eye who managed to snap a picture of the one and only time she and Bob had kissed.

Vanessa learned forward, clearly relishing getting the firsthand story. "If it was mutual, why did he resign?"

"Relationships with subordinates are against the rules at RKS."

"But this is Vegas. Surely this type of thing is common," Arjun said. Rani felt a small measure of relief to hear no judgment in his voice.

"Yes and no. RKS is a conservative firm and finding out that a male boss is having a romantic relationship with a female subordinate had to be taken seriously.

Plus our personal relationship was so new, we hadn't gotten around to filling out the required HR paperwork stating it was mutual. I'm not saying it's fair and I tried to stand up for Bob, but ultimately he decided it would be better for him to resign."

What she didn't say is that RKS would have overlooked the relationship had her ex not made a big deal about it. Navin's motivation had been to get her fired but Bob had taken the hit.

"Poor Bob. I hear he had to go to New York to find another position."

Rani had heard the same thing and it just added to her guilt.

"Sounds like the whole thing was not easy on you," Arjun said softly. She met his gaze and felt a comforting warmth flow through her.

Vanessa followed the look between them. "Well, I think I've had it with Indian food for tonight so I'll just get an Uber home." She pushed her chair back.

Arjun stood. "Nonsense. Sam will take you home and then come back to get us."

Arjun walked Vanessa to the car, then returned to their table. Rani didn't know whether to feel relieved Vanessa was gone or nervous that she was now alone with Arjun.

"You have hardly touched your food. Too spicy?" He grinned.

She smiled then shook her head. "I love spicy food, but nothing beats homemade Indian food."

His lips curved up. "Do you cook?"

*What a typical question from an Indian man.* She shook her head. "Another virtue that this Indian does not have. I'm a disaster in the kitchen. The only thing I know how to make is masala chai."

"My sisters are the same way. My mother tells them that they had better marry someone rich who can hire a cook for them, or else they'll starve."

Rani laughed mirthlessly. "That's the same advice my mother gave me. And I took it and married someone rich."

Arjun stopped mid-chew. "You're married?"

Was it wrong that she felt a tingle at the surprise and disappointment in his voice? "Divorced," she said simply, then waited. While divorce was much more common than it used to be, it was still a little taboo among Indians. And the inevitable *what happened* question was not easy to answer. *No, he did not leave me. No, he did not beat me. No, he did not have an affair.* Apparently those were the only acceptable reasons for an Indian woman to divorce her husband.

"I'm sorry to hear you had to go through something like that. It's sad that even in this day and age it's difficult to be divorced in the Indian community."

*Is this man for real?*

"It's getting late, I should head back." She didn't want to get to know Arjun any better. They'd already gotten too personal.

"What's the rush? We have to wait until Sam returns with the car anyway."

She could take an Uber. But she was supposed to be taking the client out to dinner. How could she walk out? *Be professional, get back to the contract.*

"Do you regret having dated at work?"

Rani was jolted by the non sequitur. Arjun's soft

brown eyes looked at her with such intensity that her nerves tingled.

"Yes, I do. It was the first and last time I'll ever get involved with someone at work."

Arjun stared at her for a few seconds and as much as she wanted to, she couldn't break the eye contact. It was as if he was trying to convey something without saying it out loud.

"It's getting late. Would you mind if I paid the bill, then took an Uber back to my car? I have a lot of work to do on these contract modifications."

"Don't worry about the bill. I will take care of it, but do wait for Sam. You should not be out alone at this time of night."

*Excuse me? Now there's the Indian man I was expecting.* She knew only too well what he meant. Her ex in-laws had been the same way. *Girls from good families don't go out alone at night.* Translation: *we feel more comfortable being in control of your whereabouts.*

Rani gestured for the check. Venkat pulled out a piece of paper from his apron pocket, then handed it to Arjun without a second glance at Rani.

"Dinner is on RKS," she said forcefully, holding out her hand for the bill.

"It's okay, Rani." Arjun extracted some bills from his wallet and handed them to Venkat, brushing off Rani's gestures to hand her the check.

*Well isn't that typical. Always needs to be in control.*

She pulled out her phone and tapped on the screen.

"My Uber will be here in a few minutes. Thank you for dinner, Mr. Singh. I'll send over the revised contract in the morning." She stood and walked out.

"Rani, wait!"

She resisted the urge to walk faster. Her Uber was still ten minutes away and it was pointless to get too far from her pickup location. Arjun strode up to her.

"What just happened? I feel like I offended you and I have no idea why."

She turned to face him and took a sharp breath. *He's your client, Rani. Watch it.* "Not at all, everything's fine. I just realized how late it is and I'd like to get home," she said in a high-pitched voice.

"Rani, you originally suggested we go out to Portofino's for a three-course meal. Please don't be formal with me. Just tell me what I did to upset you."

"I specifically asked to pay the bill and I don't like how you ignored me."

To his credit, he didn't smirk or say *is that all?* He placed his hand on his heart. "My apologies, Rani. My chivalry got the better of me. I don't ever let a woman pay."

"We aren't on a date. You're my client. Did it occur to you that RKS expects me to take clients out to dinner and I'll need to explain why I didn't?"

Before he could say anything, Sam pulled up to the curb next to them. "Seeing as your ride isn't here, could I do my *colleague* the courtesy of giving her a ride?"

It would be childish to resist. She nodded and slid into the plush leather seats of his Lexus. They rode to Arjun's office in silence but she was acutely aware of him next to her in the back seat. On the ride to the restaurant, Arjun had ridden up front with Sam while she and Vanessa shared the back seat. Despite the spaciousness of the car, Arjun felt too close. She could sense his breath as he exhaled, smell his spicy aftershave, feel the heat from his body. The short ride back to her car felt interminable.

There were no empty spots next to her car in the garage, so Sam pulled up a few feet away. "Thank you again, I'll be in touch," Rani said. She collected her laptop bag and had scarcely gotten her door open when Arjun appeared on her side, pulling the door wider for her. They walked to her car in silence.

As they neared her car, Rani pulled out the keys and hit the unlock button.

"You owe me forty-six dollars and twenty-two cents."

Rani turned towards Arjun. "What?"

He held out the receipt from the restaurant. "Plus whatever you would have tipped."

Rani raised her eyebrow and took the receipt. "How much did you tip?"

He smiled. "I rounded up to an even hundred."

"That's more than a hundred percent," Rani exclaimed. No wonder Venkat was so attentive.

"Venkat has a sick son. Everything he earns, he sends home to India. That's why I ignored your request."

Now she felt like shit. Smiling, he joined his hands together in a gesture of apology. His dimple struck a fatal blow to the last of her irritation.

"Mr. Singh, RKS would not approve a hundred percent tip as a business expense, so why don't I take you out to dinner another night? When might you be free?"

"How's this coming Saturday?"

*That soon?*

"Would Vanessa be available on such short notice?"

she asked stupidly, knowing full well he wasn't including her in the dinner plans.

"I think this one will just be the two of us. You pick
the restaurant, I'll get the show tickets."

"Show tickets?"

He grinned. "My favorite comic, Russell Peters, is
doing a show. I was hoping you would come with me."

Her heart jumped. *As in a date? No, that can't be
right.* "I don't think it would be appropriate for us to
see each other socially."

"We can go as colleagues, or two random Indians
who have a sense of humor and want to support a po-
litically incorrect comic."

She couldn't help but smile. "When you put it that
way, how can I say no?"

"Great, text me your address and I'll pick you up."

*This is sounding a little too much like a date.*

Rani looked at the receipt that was still in her hand.
"How did you know Venkat had a sick son?"

Arjun shrugged. "I noticed him crying outside the
restaurant one night when I stopped to get carryout. I
asked him what was wrong."

*He stopped and asked what was wrong.*

"Before you get the wrong idea about me, I'm not a
bleeding heart, just a little homesick, and Venkat reminds me of one of my favorite servants."

*A favorite servant.* Rani resisted the urge to roll her
eyes.

Arjun opened her car door. She threw her laptop
bag on the passenger seat and got in. He leaned down
through the doorway as a car tire screeched in the distance. His face was inches from hers, backlit from an

overhead light. His aftershave smelled of a sultry mix of sandalwood and spice. A five o'clock shadow darkened his face. His lips were close. *So close.* All she had to do was lean forward a few inches. She bit her lip and heard the sharp intake of his breath.

"I have to warn you, Rani, you're making me reconsider my policy about the company ink."

6>*Just when you think you understand him, he surprises you.*

# Four

"Then he just left?"

Rani heard the incredulity in her roommate and best friend Em's voice. She nodded.

"What did he mean?" Em demanded.

"If I knew, I wouldn't be asking you to translate man-speak for me."

Em took a big gulp from her can of soda and Rani smiled, amused by her friend's new lime-green hair. She was a pediatric oncology resident and she changed her hair color every time she discharged a patient. The other kids who remained on the unit picked the color. It was her way of giving them hope.

Rani held out a black dress in front of her. Em shook her head. "Do you have anything that's not black and conservative?"

Rani frowned. Sadly she didn't. It had been two years since she'd really been out on a date. *Not that this is a date.* The only clothes she had were business-appropriate.

Em went to her own room and returned with a strappy red dress. Rani shook her head. "That'll send the wrong message."

"And what message are you trying to send?"

Rani stepped into the black dress Em had rejected and studied her image in the mirror. The simple shift looked proper and boring and very businesslike. She thought of Vanessa and the other women from Arjun's office.

"I want to show him that I can be sexy. But I want to make it clear this is not a date."

Em raised a brow then walked out of the room. She returned a few minutes later and slipped a sparkly necklace around Rani's neck that fell between her breasts and handed her a pair of dangly earrings. She began pulling the pins out of Rani's chignon.

"What are you doing?" Rani protested, ineffectively batting Em's hands away.

Em fluffed Rani's hair, then pointed at the mirror.

Rani had to admit the effect was pretty good. Her shiny shoulder-length black hair fell in waves, naturally curly from being tied up all day. She put on the earrings. "You don't think this is too unprofessional?"

Em smacked her hand on her forehead. "I thought we were going for business sexy!"

Rani blew out a sigh and sat on the bed. "I should've canceled."

"Rani, it's been forever since you did something fun.

Why don't you stop overanalyzing and just go out and have a good time. You love Russell Peters. Have a few laughs, enjoy the company of a handsome, intelligent man and let things happen naturally."

"I can't let anything happen. He's a client. If I get the contract to design his full hotel, it'll set me up on the fast track to start my own firm. I can't risk all of that for…for…"

"Toe-curling sex?"

Rani nodded, too embarrassed to say it out loud.

"I've known you since high school. Not once have you done anything risky. You were a virgin when you got married. Probably the only one in our entire school. Somehow I don't see you losing your panties tonight. But if you wanted to, there's nothing wrong with it. This is Vegas. You know how the saying goes."

Rani smiled. Em placed both hands on Rani's shoulders, her slate-gray eyes serious. "Every day I deal with children who would give anything just to go outside and play, eat ice cream and do the simple things that you and I take for granted. You've been living with an enormous weight on your shoulders. First your parents' expectations, then your in-laws'. When have you ever lived? When have you done something that brings you joy?"

"It's easier said than done."

Em fluffed Rani's hair a little more. "I know you're worried about your career, but you're not in the same situation as you were two years ago. There's no one out to get you."

Before Rani could think about it any longer, there was a knock on the door. Her apartment building was too low-rent to have a working buzzer, so the residents frequently propped open the front door to the building, letting anyone off the street just walk in.

"That's Arjun. He's right on time! I need shoes!" Rani said, panicked.

"Go let him in. I'll get you heels."

Rani opened the door to find Arjun standing there, ready to take her breath away. He wore his usual perfectly cut black suit, but his shirt was unbuttoned at the collar, revealing a hint of chest hair. His face was freshly shaven and she hoped that if she stepped closer, she might catch a whiff of that intoxicating smell from last night.

"Wow, Rani, you look beautiful."

She blinked. "Um, thank you. I'm ready to go, I just need…"

She looked down to see that Em had surreptitiously placed a pair of red-and-black heels near her feet. *There is no way I can wear those shoes.* She looked around for the sensible ones she wore with her business suit and noted they were gone from their usual place.

"Your purse," Em whispered.

"Is that your flat mate?" Arjun asked.

Em stepped forward. "Emmaline Roberts. Nice to meet you."

"Arjun Singh."

"I don't want to keep you two. I know it's hard to squeeze dinner in before a show." Then, turning away, from Arjun, Em mouthed, "He's hot. Go for it."

Rani put on the red-and-black heels, wondering how long it would be before she took an embarrassing spill.

She teetered down the stairwell to Arjun's waiting

car, wondering what he must think of her. Vanessa probably did jumping jacks in her four-inch heels.

Rani had picked an upscale Malaysian restaurant for
dinner, and she filled the silence in the car by telling
him about the chef and the menu. "This particular chef
combines not just Indian, Chinese and Thai flavors but
also uses a lot of African and Arabian spices."

"It sounds right up my alley."

"I know."

"You were quite thorough in researching me."

"Everything I know about you is what you allow the
media to report."

He raised an eyebrow, and the corner of his mouth
lifted up in a look so sexy that Rani found it hard to
breathe. "That's right, Ms. Gupta."

"So, how about telling me something real."

"Well, you've read about all my favorite foods. What
you don't know is that I like cooking the dishes myself."

*He cooks?* Arjun Singh had grown up with the kind
of wealth and privilege that most people could only
dream of. He'd been surrounded by servants all his life.
She couldn't imagine him doing something as domestic
as cooking a meal.

They arrived at the restaurant and were seated immediately. Rani was pleasantly surprised since it was
a popular place and the bar was packed with waiting
customers. They were shown to a quiet table in a back
room where there were only two other couples seated.
Rani wondered if that was why they hadn't had to wait:
they were being shown to the loser seats.

Arjun didn't seem to mind, so she didn't say anything. They shared an appetizer of mango and tofu

salad, then moved on to a family-style dinner of *roti canai*, chili chicken, crispy squid and Singapore noodles. They talked about their favorite foods, movies, TV shows and books. Rani discovered that Arjun was a fellow fan of political and psychological thrillers.

They shared mango sticky rice for dessert. Arjun put his hands up when the check came and Rani deftly set down the RKS business card, guiltily realizing she'd forgotten it was a business dinner. They hadn't talked about work at all.

Arjun had secured box seats for the show, giving them a bird's-eye view of the stage, where an opening act band was playing. "What, no front row seats?" Rani quipped. Arjun shook his head. "Comedians always pick on the front row, and then your embarrassment can live in perpetuity on social media."

Rani hadn't even thought about that. "It must be really hard for you to constantly worry about the media."

He nodded.

"At the restaurant, they purposely sat us in the back room?"

He smiled sheepishly. "Before I go out, my assistant always calls the restaurant to make sure there won't be any reporters, and to secure seats in a private section, if possible."

Rani couldn't fathom living that way. "So Venkat was overseeing the VIP section yesterday?" she quipped.

"Impromptu dinners are different. And Venkat keeps an eye out for anything shady." As they settled into the conversation, Rani found herself relaxing. Truth be told, this was the best date she'd had in her life.

She mentally slapped herself. *This isn't a date, Rani!* When a waiter appeared and took drink orders from them, she asked for sparkling water. This was a work dinner, after all. *But what if it could be more than that?*

Arjun's phone buzzed just as the waiter set down their drinks. He looked at the text to see it was another one from Hema. Whatever you said to your mom didn't work. She's in full scale Diwali/engagement party planning mode. Do something! Arjun clenched his teeth. Hema was a grown woman. Why couldn't she just tell her parents she wasn't ready to get married? His phone buzzed again, this time with a text from Divya. Arjun hit the Do Not Disturb setting on his phone. He deserved a night of peace.

"Where did you disappear to?" Rani's soft voice broke through his reverie, drowning out the sound of the warm-up comedian who was introducing himself on stage. Arjun tried to give her his fake smile but stopped short when he looked into her eyes.

She reached over and touched his hand, which was on the armrest between them. Her touch was soft and delicate and immediately calmed the storm raging inside him. He dealt with thousands of problems each day and none of them twisted him up in knots like his family did.

"Are you okay?" Rani asked.

The changing stage lights threw seductive shadows across her face, and he felt himself gazing into her dark eyes. He'd always thought she was beautiful but tonight she looked spectacular. He knew she wasn't wearing a designer dress, and if he had to guess, she probably hadn't spent all day at the beauty salon getting her hair and makeup done. Yet she looked more stunning than any woman he'd ever met. Those heels that she clearly hated showed off her long, shapely legs and the way her hair framed her face made him want to weave his fingers into it. She was looking at him with such intensity, it seemed she could see into his soul.

"Just family drama," he said, surprising himself. He pulled his hand away from hers before he was tempted to take things further. Last night when he'd said goodbye in the car, he'd felt such an urgent need to kiss her that he'd almost canceled their plans tonight. He prided himself on always being in control.

He took a sip of the neat whiskey he'd ordered, hoping the raw burn down his throat would bring him back to his senses and shake loose an idea on how to deal with his family.

"Tell me about it." Rani leaned in close to him, and he caught a whiff of her vanilla scent.

*Where do I start? With Divya or Hema?* Hema was a not a problem to solve. She was an obligation he had to come to terms with. "My sister Divya has been offered a job in Jaipur and wants to take it, but that's not done in our family."

"Why not?"

He shifted in his chair.

"What I mean is, what is your parents' specific concern beyond the fact that it's not the tradition? The *parampara*?"

He looked at her in surprise. *She gets it.*

"I think they fear that if she's financially independent, she won't follow the house rules." Even as he said the words, he realized how horrible it sounded. "You have to understand that my parents are doing what they think is best for her."

"They're trying to control her."

"They are trying to protect her."

"I don't think we'll agree on that point. So what do you plan to do?"

"I'm thinking of secretly increasing her allowance. That way she can buy what she wants without having to ask my parents' permission. That's how this whole job thing started. She wanted to buy a car for herself and they questioned her spending."

Rani shook her head. "You're not understanding her."

He frowned. While he wanted Rani's perspective, she didn't know Divya. Arjun talked to Divya almost every day. How could Rani be so confident in saying he didn't understand his sister?

"Divya doesn't want to work just to buy things. She wants to work to have a sense of purpose, of independence. To do something meaningful with her life. I don't think you can appreciate what it's like for an intelligent person to sit at home all day with nothing to do. It's maddening."

"She has lots of things to do. There is staff to manage, social events to plan, charity work. My mother is always complaining about how busy she is."

"But those aren't things that satisfy a young, educated woman who doesn't want to be a socialite. She wants do something that is uniquely hers, and have control over some aspect of her life."

"It seems you're speaking from personal experience."

She nodded. "My ex-husband's family didn't have

your kind of wealth but they were comfortable. My in-laws asked me to quit my job, which I foolishly did. My days were filled with shopping and social events that I couldn't care less about. I'm guessing your sister lives a similar life. Working is not about the money, it's about independence. Of the many things I lost during my marriage, the one I lament the most is my career. I was almost at the point of making senior architect at RKS when I left. After the divorce, I had to start at the bottom of the junior level because I'd been out of the game so long. Divya doesn't want to become obsolete."

Arjun spread his hands. "So what do you suggest I do? My mother will not agree to let her get a job. I've already tried to convince her and she is firm on this point."

"What is Divya qualified to do?"

"She studied law."

Rani chewed her lip, and he found himself staring at her. "Your business is big enough that you surely need lawyers."

He nodded. "Of course. I have a couple in every city that we have a hotel."

"So hire her for your legal team in the Jaipur office."

"Jaipur is an hour away from our home."

"Do you do the commute?"

He rubbed his neck. *It could work.* "We have a trusted driver who could take her every day."

It was a nice idea. His brother, Sameer, had no interest in working for the family business, and Arjun could use a trusted person to take on some of the responsibilities of the company while he was in Vegas. He was tired of having to wake up in the middle of the night to get on the phone with someone in India.

"It's a potential solution. Thank you, Rani."

The crowd became louder as the warm-up act wrapped up and introduced Russell Peters. Rani started laughing at one of the jokes. Arjun hadn't heard it. All he could focus on was the way her mouth crinkled, and the happy sound of her giggles and laughter. He'd been with a fair number of women in the last several years; all of them had been socialites who clearly understood that he wasn't looking for an emotional attachment. His relationships were always physical. None of them had made him want to connect emotionally like this.

"Am I really more amusing than the comedian?" Rani turned to him, grinning.

He smiled sheepishly. "You certainly are more beautiful."

Her eyes widened and her mouth opened slightly. He took a breath to keep from leaning over and kissing her irresistible lips. As if reading his mind, she suddenly snapped her head back towards the stage. He took a long slug from his glass of whiskey.

*So what if we work together?* The project would be over in less than six months and he'd be returning to India to a lifetime of obligation. If she was attracted to him too, what was wrong with a brief affair? He knew how to be discreet; he would protect Rani, and make sure there would be no fallout for her at RKS. *After all, what happened in Vegas could stay in Vegas.*

# Five

The show was over but Rani didn't want the evening to end. The warm October night and the irresistible sparkle of the Vegas strip made her link her arm with Arjun's as they walked down Las Vegas Boulevard. The streets were packed with crowds spilling from all different directions, loud and clumsy and infectiously happy.

"How about a walk to the Bellagio fountains? It's about a mile," Arjun suggested.

Rani had easily done the walk before but not in killer heels. She almost refused but she didn't want the evening to end. The only thing waiting for her at home was an online movie.

As they walked, their conversation turned back to food as Rani recalled her favorite dishes at the endless eateries and hotels lining the Strip. When they got to the New York-New York hotel and casino, Arjun looked at the large Statue of Liberty dominating the fake city skyline.

"Do you think I should've built a large replica of the Taj Mahal?"

Rani laughed because she knew from the look on Arjun's face that he was joking. It was funny how in the short time she'd known him, she could already read so many of his facial expressions.

"You still can. We can add a giant dome to the roof and four pillars at the corners of the building. Then we can have it painted in a faux marble look. I could do the architectural drawings tomorrow if you like. The only thing is, you'll have to change your plans for the restaurant from a Michelin star chef to a team of short order cooks that can put out large buffets. And you'll have to change the plans for the casino. Forget the high roller tables. Think quarter slots." They both laughed at the thought. The Mahal hotel wasn't going to cater to regular tourists like most of the hotels on the strip. The casino was for serious players only. The rooms were luxurious and exclusive. The restaurant would cater to the most discerning foodies. High class all the way.

"Shit." The Bellagio fountains were in sight when Rani's heel got stuck in a pothole. Just in time, Arjun caught her from falling face-first onto the sidewalk.

"Ouch, ouch!" Her heel was wedged into the sidewalk so tight that she couldn't lift her foot out. Arjun bent down and unstrapped her shoe. She stood on one leg while he extricated her shoe from the hole. Then he half carried her to a nearby bench. He bent down on one knee and gently lifted her leg.

His warm hand on her foot sent a delicious signal right to her core.

"You're ankle is bleeding and swelling up. I'm calling Sam to come get us."

"Good idea." It didn't feel like she'd broken anything other than her pride, but her ankle was hurting. She shouldn't have worn the stupid heels.

While they waited for Sam to make his way through the clogged traffic, they watched the Bellagio fountains from afar. It was a spectacular show of water and light timed to music. Arjun put his arm around her shoulders and she leaned against him to keep the weight off the ankle. For the first time in years, Rani felt weightless.

When Sam pulled up, Arjun helped Rani half hop, half walk to the car. As soon as they were seated, Sam roared back into traffic.

"My condo isn't far from here. We will go there first and get you bandaged."

"There's no need to do that. My roommate is a doctor. I'll be better off going home."

"Your apartment is a fifth floor walk-up. No way are you hobbling up that many flights of stairs without us icing that ankle and making sure it's okay."

"Are you always this bossy?"

"Do you even have to ask? I promise I'll be a perfect gentleman."

"Is that a promise that needs to be made?"

He gave her a big smile and her resolve melted. *That dimple!*

They arrived at a shimmering glass high-rise building with yellow accents in the city center. Rani knew it was one of the most exclusive residential condos in the city. Sam pulled into an underground garage, and once again Arjun supported her as they made their way to a private elevator.

Her heart skipped a few beats as they got to his floor and he punched in a code to open the door to his condo. *I'm going to be alone with him.* In all of her naughty dreams, she had not pictured him in bed, but now that was all she could think about.

She gasped as she entered the apartment. The doors opened to a great room with thirteen-foot ceilings and a wall of windows that offered a breathtaking view of the Eiffel Tower, and the south Strip. *This is his rental?*

"Let's get you on the couch." His arm was around her, his body close to hers as he helped her across the room. His closeness made her heart flutter.

He made quick work of getting a first aid kit and cleaning and bandaging the cut on her foot. Her ankle was swollen but she rotated it and it didn't hurt.

"I don't think it's twisted. It just looks worse than it is."

He pulled an ottoman close, lifted her leg and set her foot on it. "How about you elevate it and I'll get some ice."

Arjun went into the kitchen and returned with a bag of frozen peas, which he placed on her ankle. She winced at the cold.

"This is quite a rental."

He smiled. "It belongs to a friend of mine. He's letting me use it while I'm here. The building is run like a hotel with full concierge, room service, all sorts of amenities."

"Are you going to miss Vegas when you go back to India?"

He shrugged and stared out the window. "I'm looking forward to being on my land again."

"Well, the Vegas lights are only fun for so long. I've had a hard time feeling at home here too."

"Where do you consider home?"

"California, I guess. It's where I was born and grew up."

"Why don't you feel like you belong there?"

She looked up into his honey-brown eyes. She'd never said out loud that it didn't feel like home. "I'm from a very traditional Indian family. When I went to school, my friends were American and I wanted to do the things they did but it's not the way my parents lived at home. I couldn't have boys call me, even if they were just friends. I wasn't allowed to go out after dinner, even when I was in high school. In the end I was always torn about whether I was Indian or American and no place felt like I belonged."

"Have you been to India?"

"Yes, I have some aunts and uncles in Delhi. India feels even less like home. Everyone there treats me like an NRI—nonresident Indian. To them I'm too Americanized and to my American friends I'm too Indian."

She hadn't meant for the conversation to get so serious and personal. She looked away from him towards the view.

"I guess that means you're what they call an ABCD. An American-Born Confused Desi."

She laughed at the expression, with its use of the

colloquial Hindi term for Indian people. "Yes, that's exactly what I am."

"Well the way I see it, home is a feeling. A place where you can be yourself, feel at ease, shed the persona you show the world. For now, make my temporary home yours."

He shrugged off his jacket, then rolled up his sleeves. She watched his chest muscles flex underneath his shirt and felt a little light-headed.

"Are you hungry?"

She hated to admit it, but she was. The show had run late and it had been more than three hours since they ate dinner.

"I could eat. Maybe we can order a pizza or Chinese?"

"No way." He strode over to the open kitchen and she turned so she could watch him. He busied himself taking things out of the refrigerator. "I think I have everything I need to make lamb *saag*."

Her jaw dropped. She'd shared with him that it was her favorite dish. "You're going to try and make lamb *saag* now?"

"Why not? I'm not as bad as you think. I hired one of the best chefs in India to teach me how to cook."

She still couldn't fathom it. "You have room service, and I'm sure you could hire a cook if you want. Why would you want to toil away in the kitchen?"

"So I can cook for a beautiful woman with the hopes of impressing her."

*Beautiful woman, ha! The charm sure is on tonight.* But she couldn't deny the fact that she was enjoying his attention, as fake as it might be. He was surrounded by fine-looking women every day, yet he'd made her feel like she was one in a million tonight.

"Thanks for the compliment but it's not necessary. I'm hardly in the class of women you're used to being with."

"And what class might that be?"

"Women who are tall and skinny enough to be on the cover of the Victoria's Secret catalog."

He rolled his eyes and shook his head. "That may be your idea of beauty but it is not mine." He began chopping an onion.

"What's your idea of beauty?"

He stopped what he was doing and looked straight at her. "You, Rani. You are my idea of beautiful. You're intelligent, talented, and don't need a pound of makeup or fancy clothes to make you attractive."

Her heart thumped so hard she could feel the pounding in her ears. She was glad he wasn't close to her to see her tremble at the very idea of him wanting her. Not even in her wildest fantasies did she imagine this conversation with him.

"Your idea of beauty is not only different than every man on the planet, but also every Indian. Especially every Indian." She could tell from the way he averted his eyes that he knew what she was talking about. In India, complexions ranged from almost white to almost black and the fairer a woman, the more beautiful she was considered. Growing up, she'd been told, *Rani, you are not fair, tall or slim so you must be smart if you want to marry a good man.* Her mother's words were not malicious but matter-of-fact. And they'd been echoed by every well-meaning aunt in her family.

It was a part of her culture that Rani both loved and hated. People were brutally honest. An American aunt would disingenuously reassure her if asked whether she looked fat in a pair of jeans. An Indian auntie would point out her big butt before she even asked.

"I don't view things that way. What you're referring to are the antiquated beauty standards of my parents' generation."

It was the perfect answer. One she wished she could have taped and replayed to her mother and every Indian woman of a certain generation. While the choice to marry Navin had been hers, the prejudices she had grown up with had influenced her decision-making. Navin was a successful, well-off Indian man who was much darker complected than she was. She'd liked the idea of joining a family where she was the lighter-skinned one, rather than the one who was constantly being handed skin bleaching creams.

Arjun held up a wineglass and she shook her head. She did not want to feel uninhibited with Arjun. She was already drunk on him.

"Mango *lassi*, then?"

She nodded and he retrieved a crystal glass containing the yellow beverage from the refrigerator.

She stood and gingerly put weight on her ankle. It seemed better. She made her way to the island and perched herself on one of the stools.

"Are you sure you're okay on that stool?"

She nodded and he handed her the glass.

She took a long sip and sighed with pleasure. "Wow, this might just be the best mango *lassi* I've had. Did you make this?"

He shook his head. "The head chef at one of my hotels in India made it. I had him overnight it."

"You had him mail mango *lassi* from India?" She laughed as she pictured a dripping FedEx envelope making its way across the Pacific Ocean.

"Why not? People have special meals shipped all the time."

*Normal people did not have their meals shipped across the globe. They eat mediocre takeout or go to the frozen section of their grocery store to get their exotic fix.*

He threw onions into a pan and while they sizzled, he added a bunch of spices. Then he began chopping tomatoes and garlic.

"The mango *lassi* alone is fine for me. You really don't have to go through the trouble of cooking."

"Rani, I'm trying desperately to impress you."

*He did not just say that!* She took a sip of her mango *lassi*, not trusting herself to speak. Her lips quivered on the glass and she barely tasted the cold liquid.

He added garlic and tomatoes to the pan, then some cubed lamb. The air filled with the smell of spices and sizzling meat. Rani's stomach growled as the familiar smells permeated her breath. It had been two years since she'd had her mother's home-cooked Indian meals. Two years since she'd talked to her parents.

"Is everything okay?" Arjun was looking at her over the steam rising from the pan.

She realized there were tears in her eyes. "Yes, it's just that my mom's kitchen smells like this and it's been a while since I've seen my parents."

He lifted the spatula from the pan and walked around

the island to where she was seated. "Here, try this." He blew on the spatula before holding it to her lips. She carefully took a bite. The spices tingled on her tongue.

"Mmm, yum. Maybe a touch more salt."

He took the spatula and finished the bite that was left on it. "Yes, I think you're right."

They chatted easily about the comedy show while Arjun cooked. He made some basmati rice as the meat simmered. When the lamb was almost done, he cut some spinach and added it to the pot.

While waiting for the rice to cook, Arjun checked her ankle.

"Don't worry, it's still attached to my leg."

He let his hand linger a second too long and Rani's nerves jangled. She switched to talking about the hotel, desperate to remember that he was her client. When the food was ready, he spooned some rice and lamb *saag* onto a plate and handed it to her.

"This smells amazing."

He sat on a stool kitty-corner to her and they dug in. From the first bite Rani knew she was in love. "Wow, that's the best lamb *saag* I've ever had." She closed her eyes and savored the spices. When she looked again at Arjun he was staring at her, his honey-colored eyes completely dark.

"That face you just made, that is the reason I like to cook," he said thickly.

She turned back to her food, hoping he hadn't noticed the heat in her cheeks.

Once they were finished eating, she helped him clear the dishes and began washing the pots. "Rani, my housekeeper will be here tomorrow. You should rest your foot."

"Those of us who don't have housekeepers can't stand the thought of going to bed with a dirty kitchen," she joked.

"Is that your way of saying you'd like to go to bed here?"

Her hand flew to her mouth to shove the words back in. "That's not what I meant at all."

He laughed. "I'm just joking with you."

"How about I make us some masala chai?" she offered hastily to get off the topic of her spending the night.

"You really should rest your foot."

"I'm fine!"

"I do have a soft spot for homemade masala chai."

He helped her find what she needed, then leaned over her shoulder as she added cardamom, cloves, cinnamon and milk to a pot of water. She added a touch of black pepper, keeping up a chatter about how she'd bribed a *chai wallah* in Delhi to give her his recipe. Arjun stood so close to her that if she moved an inch, she'd be touching him. *Just a tiny step back and I'll feel his solid chest against me.*

"Are you learning to make masala chai now?"

She felt him nodding. "Lamb *saag* takes a while to prepare. Masala chai is much more efficient for the purposes of impressing women with my domestic prowess."

"I don't think you need to cook to impress women. I think every woman in India would gladly marry you."

"Ah, but I'm not interested in all those women in

India. Right now I would really like for this ABCD to notice me."

*Notice him?* Her heart jumped into her throat. *The* Arjun Singh was trying to get her attention?

She took a tiny step back towards him, then turned so she was facing him. Her breasts brushed against his solid chest. A longing took hold of her, curled down her spine and lit a fire deep in her core. For just a moment, she wanted to be the woman a man like Arjun desired. To be the type of confident woman who could take control and seduce a man.

She looked up at him. Arjun's eyes widened as she lifted herself on tiptoe and touched his lips with hers. His kiss was featherlight, teasing, probing, testing. She circled her arms around his neck and opened her mouth to deepen the kiss. He obliged, letting his tongue explore her. His hands were loose around her waist. She felt the hard ridge of his desire and the molten heat in her own core. She moved against him and heard him groan, which sent a new pulse of electricity through her.

*What am I doing?* The temptation to see what he felt like had been all-consuming, but suddenly her brain kicked in. *He's a client.*

She made a sound and he slowly excruciatingly, ended the kiss. He moved his arms from her waist to her arms, unmolding their bodies, then rested his forehead on hers. "Rani." His voice was husky, and never in her life had her name sounded so sexy. *This was what it was supposed to feel like.*

But did Arjun think the kiss was special too, or was every kiss like that for India's hottest hottie?

"Oh no!" He pushed her aside just as the tea boiled

over and splashed out of the pot. He turned the gas off, getting some of the hot liquid on his hand. He grimaced and shook it off.

Rani took a breath to force her mind back to reality. The kiss with Arjun had been a fantasy, one that she couldn't indulge in again.

*What is wrong with me?* Arjun prided himself on being in control. He hadn't planned on kissing Rani, let alone letting the kiss get so intense that he was seconds away from lifting her up and carrying her to his bedroom. That wasn't his style. He liked to take things slow with a woman, and until tonight he'd never had a problem keeping his desire in check. Especially for someone he worked with.

Rani ran the faucet, grabbed his hand and stuck it under the cold water.

"I'm so sorry, I totally forgot about the tea." Rani's face was inches from his; she looked stricken.

He smiled. "For that kiss, I'd happily burn my hand again."

She opened her mouth, then let her hand fall away from his.

"Arjun, I can't."

He turned the faucet off. His hand stung but he didn't care.

Rani was putting distance between them. *Damn it. Why didn't I stop myself?* He sensed that Rani was not very experienced with men. If he felt unsettled by that one kiss, he could only imagine how jolted she must be.

She bit her lip. The nervous gesture was so sexy that he had to resist the urge to run his thumb over her lips.

"Our firm has a very strict morals clause. I can be fired for getting involved with a client. I'm sorry, our relationship has to be business only." She grabbed her jacket and put it on.

"Because your firm has a morals clause or because you aren't interested?" Since when did he need to question a woman's interest in him?

She shifted on her feet. "I don't think there's a woman in this world who wouldn't be interested in you, Arjun. But I have my reputation to consider."

"I understand your concern. But know that I'm very discreet. This would not affect our work together on the Mahal."

"I don't know…" she said uncertainly.

He stepped closer to her but didn't touch her. "Tell me that kiss was nothing. Because I'll be honest with you, I've had my share of women, and that kind of earth-shattering kiss is not common."

The hint of a smile played on her lips and he knew he had her.

"It was earth-shattering, Arjun. And if you weren't my client, I would love to see more of you. And I mean that literally and figuratively."

The intense longing in her eyes was enough to make him want to pull her close, but she crossed her arms, clearly fighting with herself. "This isn't the right time for us. Maybe after I'm done with your hotel."

*After we're done with the hotel, I'll be married.* While he and Hema had agreed to date other people before they were formally engaged, he had no intention of being with someone else once things became official between them.

He hung his head. "I'm sorry to hear that, Rani, but I understand. It'll just be business between us, then."

# Six

Rani didn't know how she managed to focus on work for the next four weeks. Her nights were spent tossing and turning as she tried not to think about that kiss, and fantasize about what more Arjun could do with his mouth.

She still hadn't gotten over the fact that Arjun Singh was attracted to her. Plain old Rani. How she'd had the fortitude to turn him down was still a mystery.

The only thing saving her was work. As lead architect, she had to do more than just come up with the designs. She had to oversee the contractors and supply vendors, and take care of a thousand details. Enough to keep her traitorous mind from wandering.

Since the night of their kiss, Arjun hadn't attended any of the meetings for the project. He'd sent Vanessa.

Each time a meeting was about to start, Rani had waited breathlessly for him and he hadn't come. She had politely asked about him only to be told that he was busy. She should've been relieved but was irritated. *Is he avoiding me? What the hell!*

She signed the last invoice on her desk and turned to her email. Despite being an architectural design firm, RKS's offices were as bland as a government building's. Her ten-foot-by-ten-foot space included a black functional desk, a gray mesh chair for her, and two guest chairs. The bookshelves were empty. With the promotion, she'd moved out of her cubicle and into the office and hadn't had time to personalize it other than to put a picture of her parents and siblings on the desk.

Her office phone rang and she answered it, expecting it to be Vanessa again. The woman called no less than three times a day.

"Rani, it's Bob."

The voice was familiar but it took Rani a second to realize it was *the* Bob. Bob Seagel. She hadn't spoken to him since he'd left RKS. The extent of their contact had been the occasional comment on a Facebook post.

"Bob, this is a surprise. How are you?"

"I'm great, Rani, how are you?"

She bit her lip. Why was Bob calling her out of the blue? "Fantastic. I finally made senior architect and am leading the remodel on the Mahal hotel. It's keeping me busy."

"I heard. Congratulations! That's actually why I'm calling. A Vanessa Knott called me asking about you."

Rani straightened.

"She made it sound like they hadn't fully signed

with RKS and she knew you'd worked for me and was checking a reference. I saw right through her of course. Every major firm in the country knows RKS managed to win the contract for the Mahal."

*That witch! What is she playing at?*

"What did you tell her?"

"That you're the best architect I've ever worked with. She kept digging, though, trying to get at our personal relationship, but I didn't give her anything."

Rani's mouth was dry. "Bob, I appreciate you looking out for me. You left so fast two years ago we never got a chance to talk. I want you to know that I tried to stand up for you, to let them know you did nothing wrong. There's not a day that goes by that I don't feel terrible about what happened to you because of me. I'm so sorry for…"

"Rani, stop."

Rani bit her lip. She deserved whatever harsh things he had to say to her.

"I know you tried to protect me. Me leaving had nothing to do with our relationship."

*What!* "Then why did you resign in such a hurry?"

Bob sighed. "Ian Rabat wanted me out. And not because of you. That was just a pretext. He offered me a really lucrative severance package to leave right away so he could promote Delia."

"What? Why would he go to such lengths to promote her? She started a year before I did." What Rani didn't say is that Delia wasn't even that good. Despite her years of experience, her designs were bland and her technical expertise was dated.

"Oh, you don't know? Delia is Ian Rabat's daughter from an affair he had almost forty years ago."

Rani gasped. For all the sanctimonious advice Delia gave her about morals, she'd gotten the promotion because she was the boss's illegitimate daughter.

"I found out when I was digging around for why Ian wanted me gone. Turned out that Delia was planning to leave for another firm so Ian needed to find a way to promote her so she'd stay."

"And you agreed to this?"

"It was a good deal for me. And he hooked me up with a lucrative position at my current firm. But one of the conditions Ian had was that he wanted everyone to think I left because of you so Delia wouldn't suspect he was pulling strings to get her promoted."

"Does she know she's his daughter?"

"Yes."

Suddenly exhausted, Rani leaned back in her chair. "I wish you'd told me two years ago."

Bob was silent. "I should have. At the time I was thinking very selfishly. Ian's wife doesn't know about Delia so he asked me to keep it quiet. I'm sorry you've been carrying the guilt around for so long, Rani. I would've told you if I knew you'd taken it so hard."

"Well, thank you for telling me now. You can count on my discretion."

"Oh, you don't have to be discreet. Vanessa was nice enough to tell me the rumors Ian spread around Vegas once I left. He's ruined my reputation in that entire town. By the way, watch out for Vanessa. After she called, I asked around about her. She's Vegas all the way. Always after something better for herself."

*That's rich coming from you.*

Rani somehow found the words to politely end the call. Bob promised to keep in touch, though she had no intention of staying friends with him. *All that time feeling guilty about Bob, standing up for him no matter how detrimental it was to my reputation, and he's only been looking out for himself.* Her entire life had been spent fulfilling other people's needs. First her parents', then her in-laws', and then RKS's. She'd let the company use her. She was done with that. It was time for her to get what she wanted, to take control of her life. She was going to do something for herself.

# Seven

It had been another night spent tossing and turning. Despite cranking the AC so high that Em had threatened to throw her out, Rani woke up hot and tortured with the feel of Arjun's kiss burned into her soul.

She'd written a terse email to him yesterday asking whether he knew Vanessa had called Bob about her. His response had come immediately to ask whether they could move today's owners condo walk-through to seven o'clock in the evening. Vanessa had emailed to say she wouldn't be coming.

Rani was proud of how the condo had turned out. RKS had allowed her to call in every contractor favor they were owed, not because they were trying to help her, but because they wanted to secure the contract to design the rest of the hotel, including its five hundred guest rooms, the conference rooms and the casino. Every architectural firm in Vegas was still courting Arjun and RKS didn't want to lose out.

She looked around the room one last time. She had asked the contractors to leave so she could take the meeting alone with Arjun. There was a knock on the door just as the clock struck seven.

Her heart thundered. She checked her reflection in the antique mirror in the foyer. She had splurged and bought herself a skirt suit with a stylish short jacket, and paired it with a sleeveless crimson blouse with a deep V-neck. She took a breath and opened the door.

And there he was! Dressed in jeans and an open collared shirt, Arjun looked effortlessly hot.

"Mr. Singh," she said with a purposefully mischievous tone, "I'm glad this meeting is worth your time." Rani would never have spoken to another client that way, but a familiarity hummed between them as he gave her a dimpled smile.

"Ms. Gupta." His tone was measured but his eyes unabashedly traveled the length of her body. And just like that, eating ramen noodles for a week to afford the new clothes was worth it.

She waved him inside. The antique mirror reflected the *jaali* wall that separated the foyer from the great room. A staircase led to the upper level with the bedrooms, which had a balcony overlooking the large living area and kitchen below.

He cleared his throat. "I'm sorry I haven't been able to attend our meetings. I ran into an issue with the gaming commission that's taken up my time."

"No apologies necessary. Vanessa is highly capable. Why didn't she come?"

"I suspended her, and am thinking of firing her."

Rani's hand flew to her mouth. "Not on my account, I hope? I didn't mean for her to lose her job, I just wanted to know whether you had put her up to it." Though if she was honest with herself, she never suspected Arjun would have done something like that. She'd wanted him to put Vanessa in her place.

"Of course not. And I don't allow my staff to behave that way."

Rani took a step back at his tone. "It isn't bad enough to fire her."

"She called your former boss to get dirt on you. I suspect it's because she was jealous. It was highly unprofessional."

"Why would she be jealous of me?"

Arjun rolled his eyes. "Because she could see I was interested in you, Rani. She called me on it after our dinner at Delhi Dhaba."

"And what did you say?"

"I told her it was none of her business. And speaking of business, let's get through ours, shall we?"

Rani's heart sank at his crisp tone. "Okay, then. As you can see, we have the main living areas finished. Upstairs, only the master bedroom is finished, but the other four will have the same look and feel."

He ran his hand over the wood carvings in the antique mirror frame, then walked to the living room. RKS had an excellent interior decorating team, but Rani had overseen every selection here. Divans upholstered in a rich royal-blue-and-silver pattern lined the walls underneath the balcony overhang. In the center of the room were two long couches facing each other with two large armchairs on either side forming a square. Silver hammered coffee and end tables provided an accent. The floors were a dark hand-scraped wood. Beyond the living room, the open kitchen had copper pots offset by antique white cabinets with brass handles and quartz counters. The furniture was minimal but traditional.

Arjun walked through the space, examining each piece of furniture, light fixture and decoration. Rani stood back, enjoying the silent smile that played on his lips when he touched a carved wood elephant that was her favorite piece. She should've been anxious about whether he liked her work but she was enjoying the luxury of watching his athletic figure flex and bend as he examined things. Was it really wrong to want him? Just once, maybe twice? To feel like a woman sexy enough for a man like him?

She cleared her throat. "How does the space feel?"

There was no hesitation in his reply. "Like home."

She smiled. "Your home maybe. My home has Ikea furniture and a stove from the seventies."

He smiled. "You're right. My house does have extraordinary luxuries. But what I mean is the colors, the fabrics and the wood. It all reminds me of Rajasthan. Thank you, Rani. This is what I wanted, the feel of my home."

"I can't even imagine the astronomical price you will charge for this condo."

"I don't plan to rent it out."

Rani tilted her head. "After what you've spent on this?" Arjun's budget for the owners condo was double the typical amount per square foot at similar luxury hotels. Rani assumed it was an investment he'd make up by using it to attract high rollers to the casino. How else was he going to make money on this extravagant unit?

"This is for me. For my sanity when I need to be here."

"So you won't live in India?"

"India is my home. It's where my family is and where my life will continue to be. I will never leave there. I can't imagine anyplace else being home. This is my…" he clicked his fingers as if searching for the right word "…my…"

"Escape?"

A wistful smile crossed his lips, and he looked so lost that Rani stepped towards him and touched his arm to bring him back. He smiled down at her. "Yes, my escape." He met her gaze. "Rani, you've made this as close to home as I could possibly feel. It's beyond my expectations."

His voice was thick and her heart filled with joy. Arjun's praise was hard to come by and she was exhilarated by the fact that she'd met his exacting standards for a space that was so personal to him. She released a long held breath. For years she'd been beaten down, first by Navin convincing her that she was screwed up inside, and then Delia making her doubt her abilities to lead this project. It was nice to hear someone build her up rather than cut her down.

"Shall we see the bedroom?"

Her words hung in the space between them. She focused on his lips as her nerves tingled and sparked. *He's only here for four and a half more months. This wouldn't be anything permanent. Something just for me.* It was a chance to explore a side of herself that had never surfaced before. What was wrong with that?

"I don't need to see any more. I think you've earned your firm the contract for the rest of the hotel."

Rani pulled out of her salacious thoughts and grinned at him, silently whooping with joy. The commission from this contract would put her on the path to opening her own firm.

"Before you hand me the keys to the hotel, are you sure you don't want to see the master bedroom?"

His smile flickered. "I'll see it later."

"Without me?" She couldn't keep the disappointment out of her voice. This entire project was her baby. Yes, the great room was an example of her best work, but the bedroom was her masterpiece. She'd personally picked out the sheets for the bed. Egyptian cotton.

He shook his head. "I should get going."

Rani couldn't believe what she was hearing. Where did he have to go? It wasn't even eight o'clock yet. "Arjun, it'll only take a minute. I've been killing myself trying to get it ready for tonight. The least you can do is come see it."

He stepped back from her and shook his head. "I told you that it would just be business between us. Rani, I cannot walk into a bedroom with you and keep that promise."

# Eight

*So he still feels it.* A frisson of excitement sparked through Rani. One way or another, she was getting him into that bedroom.

"Mr. Singh, you assured me that your personal feelings would not affect our working relationship." Rani put the right amount of force in her voice.

He sighed, then swore under his breath. "Right. But what do you want me to do? You are doing a fantastic job with my hotel. In fact, you're the only one that can achieve the vision I have for this hotel and more. You just proved it with what you've done here. I want you to finish my hotel, but…" He took a heavy breath. "I have not stopped thinking about you, and that's why I've been avoiding you."

Her heart was doing cartwheels. *I'm not the only one*

*who's obsessed with that kiss.* It made sense for her to swoon over him, but the fact that he—a man who could have any woman he wanted—was thinking about her was just too heady.

"Follow me, we're going to the master bedroom."

She didn't wait for him as she walked to the corner staircase that led to the upper level. He soon caught up to her but didn't say a word as she opened the hand-carved double doors. She had planned to point out how the carvings depicted the homecoming of Lord Rama, the event from Hindu mythology that formed the basis for Diwali. As the story went, the festival of lights came to be when Rama returned victorious after a battle against evil and all of the households in his kingdom lit *diyas* or candles to illuminate the way for him. She remembered from an interview she'd read that Diwali was Arjun's favorite holiday. The doors had cost more than her annual income but she knew Arjun would appreciate the craftsmanship. Now she breezed past them into the master bedroom.

It consisted of a main room, a luxurious bathroom suite and a sitting area. A four-poster bed with rich velvet drapes was the centerpiece of the space. Large windows along one wall glittered with the lights of the Vegas Strip. The windows had been finished with built-in privacy shades that could be opened and closed with the push of a button.

She turned to him, expecting him to explore the room like he had downstairs. She'd handpicked every piece of furniture, including the antique silver side tables, a richly upholstered chaise longue, a couple of well-placed chairs, and a TV cleverly hidden behind a painting that slid aside by remote control.

But Arjun wasn't looking at the room. His eyes were on her. Dark and penetrating.

"A month ago I was sure that I didn't want to get personally involved with you," she said tentatively. She bit her lip, trying to formulate her next words.

"But now?" His voice was thick, the anticipation heavy.

Rani had done a lot of thinking in the wake of Bob's confession. She was done blaming herself; she had done nothing wrong. She hated working at RKS. Her stock in the company had risen and she realized that the respect she was getting now should have been hers all along. Word was already spreading that she'd won Arjun's business for RKS, and firms were making subtle overtures towards her. With Arjun giving her the contract for the full hotel, she had even more power in the company. If they wanted to throw the morals clause at her, let them.

She met his searing gaze, her chin up, her shoulders square. "Now I want to feel the way I did when you kissed me the first time."

He made a guttural sound. "You need to say the words, Rani. Do not play with me. Tell me what you want me to do to you." His voice slid over her like hot fudge on a sundae. It melted any last doubts she had.

"I want you. I need you to make love to me." *Who is this talking?* Rani didn't know where the words had come from. She'd never spoken to a man like that. Not even in her wildest Arjun fantasies.

He didn't waste a second. He closed the distance between them, cupped her face in his hand and brought his mouth down on hers. This time the kiss was exactly as she expected it to be, hard and bruising. She stood on her toes to get even closer to him and he bent down further. Every nerve inside her was alive, begging for his touch. She ran her hands along the muscles of his back, scratching lightly with her fingers, letting him know that she was ready for more. He groaned into her mouth and she pressed her body into his.

*Oh, he's definitely feeling it too.*

Arjun had meant to kiss her lightly and sweetly, something to tempt her into what he really wanted from her. But his lips had a mind of their own. They pressed against hers with naked need. His tongue darted out and plunged into her mouth, hungry for a taste of her. She fit perfectly into him and moaned when she felt his arousal. He shifted to mold himself to her body, all the while hungrily plundering her mouth. He dropped his hand from her cheek and ran it down her shoulder and over her waist. Her hands were in his hair, tugging and pulling. He reached underneath her blouse and cupped her breast through the lace of her bra. It was soft and round and heavy, her nipple taut.

He wanted her. Bad. Unlike his brother, who partied and had one-night stands, Arjun enjoyed short, discreet affairs. He always selected intelligent, career-minded women who understood from the start that their relationship would be short-lived and most importantly, needed to be kept private. His girlfriends were secure enough in their lives not to fall in love with him. Did

Rani meet the last criterion? Could she be with him without losing her heart?

A plaintive moan escaped her throat and the sound was desperately sexy. "Are you sure you want to do this here? Like this?" He half hoped she'd ask him to stop. When he'd imagined their first time—something he didn't care to admit doing—he'd envisioned champagne and fine chocolates. And room service breakfast. Though now that he was in this room, there was poetry in christening it with the woman who was making his dream hotel come true.

She reached into her jacket pocket and took out a condom. "I want this, Arjun." Her voice was barely over a whisper. He took the foil packet from her hands and strode over to the nightstand, barely noticing the Calacatta marble top. He turned to her with a smile on his face. "I don't think we'll be needing that for a while. I plan to make sure you are good and ready before we get to that part."

Her mouth fell open and her eyes went wide. The prim shirt did little to conceal the peaks of her nipples as they thrust forward.

He shrugged off his jacket and draped it on the bench at the foot of the bed. Rani stood frozen, so he stepped behind her and kissed the back of her neck, enjoying the little shiver she gave up. He kissed her earlobe as he pushed her jacket down over her shoulders. He flung it onto the bench next to his. Then he lifted her shirt over her head and took it off. She gasped as he cupped her breasts, teasing her nipples through the thin lace of her bra. He unzipped her skirt and let it fall to the ground.

"Um, there is one thing I need to tell you."

He took a breath. She'd been married before so he knew she wasn't a virgin. That was a line he refused to cross. There were plenty of women in India who still believed in saving themselves for their husbands and he would never be the man to take that away from them.

"I've only been with one man."

Arjun's hands stilled. Somehow that didn't surprise him. But it did complicate things. Would sex mean more to her than it did to him?

*Will she expect something from me?*

"Do you want me to stop?"

"No!"

She turned around so she was facing him and stepped close enough that her breasts were touching his chest. "I just wanted you to know that I'm not very experienced in how to treat a man in bed."

He touched her cheek. "I don't think you need to worry about my pleasure." He looked pointedly down to where his arousal was plainly visible. "But you do understand that there is no long-term future for the two of us. This is temporary."

She nodded vehemently. "I'm not looking for a relationship. I've done the Indian marriage and in-laws thing and it's not for me. My career is my focus right now."

He should have been relieved, yet for some reason her words twisted in his heart. What did it matter anyway? She was on the same page as him, and that's what was important.

"Good, let's show you what you've been missing." He moved his hands to her bottom, then lifted her into his arms, causing her to squeal in surprise. He walked over to the bed and set her down. He went to unclasp her bra but her hands flew to her breasts.

"You are beautiful, Rani."

She reached over and flipped the light switch on the wall, throwing the room into darkness. There was enough light from the windows that he could see Rani perched on the edge of the bed, her arms protectively around her chest. She truly was beautiful with just the right amount of womanly curves that stoked the fire already raging through his body.

He didn't need to ask her to know that her sexual experience hadn't been great. It was obvious from the way she fought with herself, responding to him with open desire, then shutting down just as quickly. *What's the right move here?* She was like a newborn kitten, eager to explore but afraid to approach. He was used to women who were sexually liberated, who told him how to deliver them pleasure. Women who knew what they wanted and weren't shy about it. But with Rani, he'd have to figure out what drove her wild without scaring her away.

He was up for the challenge.

*What was I thinking?* Rani had waxed, bought lacy underwear and packed a condom. Actually, a whole box of condoms. She'd spent a month of sleepless nights fantasizing about Arjun running his hands over her, imagined his naked body pressed against hers, his mouth ravaging her. In the cold light of day she'd had agonizing arguments with her heart about whether the risk was worth it. Finally she came to the conclusion that Arjun wasn't from Las Vegas, or even an American. He wasn't going to be around long-term so she didn't have to think about what life with him would be like. This project would be over soon enough. Surely she could indulge herself, especially now that she knew Delia's hypocritical secret.

So tonight she'd been prepared, physically and mentally, for the kind of toe-curling sex Em talked about. And here she was, her entire body tingling in anticipation of his next touch, and yet she was letting Navin's words worm into her thoughts.

*Some women don't like sex. I think you're one of them.*

Arjun came towards her and placed his arms on either side of hers. The lights from the Strip glimmered in his eyes. "Are you okay? We can stop now if you want."

*Why does he keep asking me that?* Was her nervousness that obvious? Or was he having doubts himself? In response, she began unbuttoning his shirt. It was time to see how well her mind had conjured his naked body in her dreams. When she was done with the buttons he shrugged off the shirt and leaned forward again, placing his palms on the bed. His face was a mere inch away from hers. She looked straight into his blazing eyes and unbuckled his belt. Very carefully, she unzipped his pants, touching his length with her hands as she went. He closed his eyes and took a sharp breath. She pushed his boxer briefs down with his pants and he kicked them off. She got her first look at him in the shadows and wished she hadn't turned the lights off. *Magnificent.*

Her imagination had not done him justice. Dark hair covered his chest. His legs were pure muscle, his arousal long and thick. She licked her lips, her mind completely emptying of all coherent thought. He stepped towards her, bent his head and kissed her. This time she kissed him back with abandon, sucking on his tongue the way she wanted to suck on him, letting him know just how much she ached for him.

He ran his hand down her body, stopping to caress her breasts, then continued down to her stomach and— *oh, thank you*—right between her legs. Her bud was throbbing and his finger found it with ease, applying just the right amount of pressure to make her moan and feel a welcome rush of heat. For once in her life, she knew exactly what she wanted. She pushed her black lace panties down, then took hold of Arjun and guided him towards her. Just when his tip touched her swollen bud, he put his hands on top of hers and retreated.

A moan of protest escaped her lips.

"Not so fast."

She didn't have the words to tell him she couldn't wait, that the heat coursing through her was so intense that she would internally combust. He gently pushed her shoulders back until she was flat on the bed. When he nestled his head between her legs, she gasped. His tongue found her throbbing need and circled and sucked it. Then his fingers pushed into her gently, slowly, *too damn slowly*. She rocked against his finger, letting him know that she wanted it faster, harder.

"Rani..." His voice was thick and husky and so wonderfully sexy but all she could think about was getting his mouth back on her. She lifted her head and weaved her fingers through his hair, grabbing a fistful. He got the message and pushed three fingers inside her. Suddenly an overwhelming crescendo seized her body, giving her that sweet release she'd been thirsting for. Her mind and body exploded and she didn't know how much time passed before she came down from the stratosphere and back into the real world.

*Wow.* She thought she'd had orgasms before but it was like comparing the intensity of a candle flame to that of a roaring fire. *I've really been missing out.* Once again, Navin's voice pierced her head, telling her that she was too reserved in bed, too unwilling to experiment. *Too cold.* She pushed Navin firmly out of her mind. She wasn't going to let him spoil this glorious moment for her.

She propped herself on her elbow to find Arjun laying a trail of kisses up her belly toward her breasts. He took one nipple in his mouth and teased it with his tongue. *Whoa, whoa, whoa.* The inferno inside her was ramping back up. His tongue was doing things that re-stoked that very delicious but raging fire deep within her. By the time he made it to her neck, she was writhing underneath him. A smile played on his lips as he lifted his head and looked at her. *That damn sexy mouth.* She reached up and kissed him, smelling herself on his lips. The scent drove her wild, as did the feel of his hardness against her. She reached between them and grabbed him. He put his hand on hers and stilled her. *Am I doing it wrong?*

"Rani, if you'd like me to last a little while longer, you need to stop touching me."

*What? I'm affecting him?*

"I want you inside me. Now." She colored at the nakedness of her words.

He groaned and lifted himself off her, grabbing the condom off the nightstand. He slipped it on as she watched. She expected him to plunge right into her but he returned his lips to her breast, suckling and teasing. She raised her pelvis, an open invitation, but he kept torturing her with his mouth and then his fingers. Finally, unable to take it any longer, she grabbed him and thrust upward, so he was inside her. She clenched against him. He rocked faster and faster, matching her rhythm. Then suddenly it came, the explosion that lit her world. Even more intense than the last, it took a while for her to come down from the high.

When she opened her eyes, Arjun was leaning toward her, his forehead touching hers. *Did he enjoy it? Did he finish?* She'd been so focused on her own pleasure that she hadn't paid attention to his. Now she noticed that he was soft inside her.

He lifted his head and dropped a gentle kiss on her lips.

She wanted to tell him how much this had meant to her. To know that she was capable of enjoying sex like a normal woman. That nothing was wrong with her. She could arouse a man like him and have the kind of mindblowing orgasms that other women always talked about.

Most of all she wanted to thank him for showing her that she wasn't broken.

*7>He will rock your world. If you let him.*

# Nine

"Well." Arjun spoke first. "We can't sleep here tonight."

She nodded. "The workers may show up really early to start on the other bedrooms. Um…it was a great. I guess I'll see you around."

He laughed and pulled her close. "Oh no, you're not getting away that easy. I'm spending the night with you." Her heart kicked at the fierceness in his voice. "We will go back to my place."

Rani wanted to object to the plan but the thought of spending the night with him was too tempting.

They dressed quickly, then made the bed together. He stealthily held her hand on the way down to the almost completed lobby, then let go when they reached the circular driveway out front where Sam was waiting with the car. She appreciated Arjun's caution; the last thing she needed was for RKS to suspect what had just happened between them. While she wasn't so worried about losing her job anymore, she didn't want people to think she got the hotel contract because she was sleeping with Arjun.

She followed his car and parked in the visitor's lot. He met her in the lobby. As soon as they got inside his condo, he kissed her. She knew without a doubt that he was ready to make love to her again and that knowledge gave her a rush. It had been such a struggle to arouse Navin; she'd constantly felt inadequate.

In one night, Arjun had elevated her confidence, in and out of bed. A month ago a promotion was the best she could've hoped for with her career. Now, a world of possibilities lay at her feet. All because Arjun believed in her. When she was done with his hotel, all of Vegas would know her name. And this time for the right reasons.

Then doubt snaked through her.

He began undressing her but she stopped him. "Arjun, I need to ask. Did you give me the hotel contract because you'd hoped we would get together tonight?"

He frowned at her. "How could you ask me that, Rani? I gave it to you because you earned it. You did an extraordinary work with the owners condo. And I had no idea you were even interested in us getting together. You did a good job convincing me I was not worth your time."

She laughed. "Not worth my time? You've been consuming my every dream since we met."

He grinned, and she kissed that dimple that had been driving her mad.

"Well then, how about we make some more dreams come true." And with that, he led her into the bedroom.

When she woke in the morning, all she could think about was how unreal it was to be in Arjun's bed and not starting at the popcorn-textured ceiling of her apartment. She rolled over, expecting to find Arjun, but the bed was empty. She sat up. He wasn't in the room. She looked for a note on the nightstand but there was none.

*Is our time over?* She quickly wrapped a sheet around her and raced downstairs to the great room. A room service cart next to the dining table where Arjun, dressed in a bathrobe, was seated with a cup and saucer in his hand. She let out a breath.

"Good morning." He grinned when he saw her. "What do you eat for breakfast?"

"Usually it's coffee and an oatmeal bar."

"Well, today you have your choice." He waved to the cart where there were no fewer than ten dishes covered by silver domes.

She gasped. "That's enough food to feed half the building."

"Well, I didn't know what you liked, so I ordered one of everything through room service. There's omelets, French toast, eggs Benedict, pancakes, Belgian waffles, oatmeal…"

Room service was a luxury she didn't allow herself even when she traveled for work on an expense account. The very thought of how much all this food must've cost made her head spin.

"Okay, let me get some clothes on."

"How about a bathrobe? It'll save me some time when I take it off later. There's one for you in the bedroom."

A shiver of anticipation went through her as she went and got the bathrobe, then joined him at the table.

"I don't have any morning meetings. How about you?" Arjun poured her a cup of coffee as she lifted the domes off the breakfast dishes.

"My first meeting is in an hour and a half, but I have to go home and change. I can't show up in the same clothes I was wearing yesterday."

"What size do you wear?"

"Um…none of your business."

He rolled his eyes. "There are some nice stores downstairs in the building complex. Let me call down to the concierge."

Rani stared as he called and got connected to the store he wanted. "Yes, this is Mr. Singh in P241. I need you to send up a few complete business outfits for my guest to select from. I'll give you a credit card now for anything she decides to keep."

He handed the phone to her. "I'll give you some privacy."

*Was he for real? Did he really expect her to order clothes like it was room service?*

"Rani?"

She realized he was still holding the phone. As soon as he handed it to her, he disappeared upstairs. The woman on the other end efficiently asked her about size, color preferences and whether she preferred any designers. *Designers?* Her clothes came from discount department stores.

She hung up the phone and found Arjun. "I'm not letting you buy me clothes," she said.

"Why not?"

"Because I'm not one of those women who lets a man buy her things and tell her what to wear." She crossed her arms and a minute of silence passed between them.

"It's not that, Rani. I just figured that it'll give us more time together. Every minute I get to spend with you is precious." He touched her arm and her heart squeezed. It was a sweet gesture and the words were even sweeter, but a part still stung. Every minute together was precious because they wouldn't have too many. She knew this was temporary and was really okay with it when all it was about was hot and lusty sex. But his tenderness was something else.

She shook her head. "Let's not waste time arguing over this. I need to leave in forty minutes."

He opened his mouth to object but then gestured to the dining table instead. They dug into the scrumptious breakfast.

"Tell me about your family," he asked after a minute of silence.

A piece of egg stuck in her throat and she coughed. "What do you want to know?"

"How about telling me more about your siblings."

She relaxed and a smile spread on her face. "My brother, Sohel, is two years younger than I am. He's trying to break into Hollywood as a screenwriter and director. My sister, Anaya, is much younger. She's still a teenager. What about your siblings?"

She already knew he had three sisters and a brother but she wanted to see how he described them.

He took a sip of his tea. "Well, my brother, Sameer, is three years younger than me and is proving to be a handful. We are so careful about our media image and he is constantly getting in trouble. I have a budget just to pay off reporters, a full time IT guy to sanitize his social media accounts, and an entire PR team that monitors all the news outlets."

His family did do a good job of keeping the dirty laundry under wraps but she didn't realize how much it took. "And your sisters? Are they just as much trouble?"

He sighed. "Divya, Karishma and Naina. They are harder to handle than Sameer. My mother is constantly calling me about some issue with them."

"Like what?"

"Well, yesterday, just before I got to the hotel, she called because Karishma and Divya snuck out of the house to go to a nightclub with their friends and Naina, who is the youngest, put pillows under their bedsheets to cover up for them."

Rani tensed. "Why did they have to sneak out?" She knew that his sisters were only a few years younger than him. Definitely old enough to be independent.

"Because it's not safe for *girls* to be out late at night by themselves in India."

Rani set down her fork a little harder than she intended and it clanked on the plate. "But it's okay for the *boys* to go out late?" Her tone was sharp but she didn't regret it.

He looked up. "It's different in India. Police enforcement is not what it should be and harassment is not punished the way it is in America so the bad elements are a little more aggressive."

She was well aware of the horrifying statistics regarding women's safety but it was not an excuse to curtail their freedoms.

"And do you know how many men get murdered every night around the world? No one uses that as an excuse to lock them at home at night."

He opened his mouth, then closed it. "You're right. I know how chauvinistic it sounds. My parents are very traditional. There are rules in our house that have existed for generations. And yes, they are sexist, but I have to choose the battles I fight. My role in the family is to run the business. My battle with my parents has been to expand outside of India—they were very reluctant to go that route. But one of the benefits is that it will open up so many opportunities for my sisters to experience the world."

*Your parents sound as bad as my ex in-laws.* Rani would never say the words out loud to him; it wasn't her business. They weren't in a relationship. She had fought her own battles, and paid the price for her freedom. What did she care what Arjun's family was like? It wasn't as if they were ever going to meet.

He leaned forward and placed his hand on hers. "I know my parents are old-fashioned. It's something I deal with every day in our house. I'm working on them, one day at a time." He smiled. "Luckily they are far away and the only thing we need to worry about right now is how to delay your first meeting."

She sighed, feeling herself give in to his charm once again. After all, what did she care about his family? She wasn't going to marry him. This was just a casual affair.

# Ten

Arjun rubbed his temples. He'd been hoping to see Rani tonight but it didn't look like he'd make it out of the office before midnight. He was having trouble with his liquor license in addition to the red tape being thrown up by the gaming commission. It was the usual headaches that came with opening a hotel. Whether it was India or America, the last-minute troubles were the same. He'd hired a Las Vegas firm to make sure the right palms were greased and the appropriate people wined and dined, but he had to personally show face and kiss a few rings to make it all work. He half suspected that since he'd used the gaming commission as an excuse not to return to India for the Diwali holiday, effectively postponing his engagement, it was the universe's way of making him pay.

He couldn't stop thinking about Rani. He'd only seen her once since their first night together. He'd taken her out to dinner at an exclusive Japanese restaurant on the outskirts of the city. The food was amazing, and her face glowed in the soft lights.

They'd talked about politics, religion, even his problems with the gaming commission. Normally Arjun kept to superficial topics with his dates, like food and travel. It was his stress-relief time, when he didn't have to think, plan, solve a problem or make an impossible decision. But with Rani, they lapsed naturally into meaningful conversations. He asked her opinions about how to resolve the problems he was having with the hotel and she offered solutions and helped him think through thorny issues. She was a good strategist and he liked talking things over with her.

He looked at his calendar again to see if there was something he could move to make time for Rani. While he enjoyed the company of women, he fit them in during holes in his schedule. He never arranged his meetings around them. But Rani was special. He wanted more time with her, in and out of bed. It was the last time he'd get to be with a woman because he wanted to be, not because he had to.

His mother had made it very clear that she was planning the wedding as soon as the hotel was done and she would not accept any more excuses from him. Hema was sending him daily text messages freaking out. He had finally told her that she had to accept the inevitable just like he did.

His assistant buzzed to let him know that Rani was

downstairs and he asked for her to be sent up immediately.

"This is a nice surprise." He greeted her from behind
his desk. His office walls were all glass and he didn't
want to give his staff a show.

She smiled and took a seat opposite him. Her de-
meanor was professional but her eyes glinted with excitement. "I have the final designs for the guest rooms.
Your team has already approved them but I wanted an
excuse to see you." On Rani's advice, Arjun hadn't fired
Vanessa, but he had read her the riot act and she'd been
much more pleasant to work with.

"I'm glad you came. I have yet another dinner with
the gaming commission tonight."

She held up a brown bag. "Then how about lunch
with me?"

He smiled. "That depends on what you brought me."

"The best drunken noodle you'll ever have. This Thai
food truck near me is amazing, just the right amount
of spice and heat."

He smiled. *Just like you, Rani. The right amount of
spice and heat.*

She took out a container and handed it to him with
a plastic fork. He stared at it, the foil tin with the paper
lid stinging him with a long buried memory.

"Is something wrong?"

He shook his head. "The last time I ate out of a container like this was eleven years ago."

Her face fell and she set the container on the table.
"I'm sorry, I should've thought about the fact that you're
not used to eating food out of plastic."

He shook his head. "It's not that. It reminds me of

this time in Mumbai with my ex-girlfriend. It didn't end well."

Rani tilted her head, her eyes begging him to tell her more.

He sighed. Why was he thinking of Lakshmi now? The last time he had talked about her was five years ago, when he'd agreed to marry Hema.

"I'm so sorry. That must have been so painful for you." Rani extended her arm across the table and put her hand on his.

"I was going to marry her. Her parents didn't approve and neither did mine so we were going to elope." He waited for the familiar ache to settle into his heart but it didn't come.

"Why didn't the parents approve?"

"Hers did not approve because they knew my parents would never accept her and they were worried that I'd dump her. Mine took issue with the fact that Lakshmi came from a poor, unknown family."

"Ah, truly the makings of a Bollywood film."

He smiled. "We thought so too when we decided to elope. We were meeting in Juhu Beach to plan the details. I stopped at her favorite restaurant to pick up *hakka* noodles. We were sitting on the sand eating out of containers exactly like those." He pointed to the takeout food she'd brought. "Then she broke my heart."

Rani didn't say anything, giving him the space to tell his story.

"She decided she didn't want to marry me."

"Why not?" Rani's voice had the same incredulous tone his had when he'd asked the question of Lakshmi.

"That day she'd auditioned for a role in a Bollywood film and she was offered the part. It was her life's dream."

"I understand such a profession wouldn't have been acceptable in your family, especially eleven years ago, but was it worth letting go of the woman you loved?"

He sighed. "She never gave me the chance to make that decision. That role had been offered to her on the condition that she leave me. My mother orchestrated it. Ma challenged me with the idea, and not in a million years did I think Lakshmi would take that offer so I told my mother to try it. I wanted to prove to Ma that our love was real. But Lakshmi came to tell me that it was her big Bollywood break and she couldn't give it up for me."

Rani bit her lip. "How could your mother do that to you?"

He bristled at her tone. "My mother has always had my best interest at heart."

Rani's lips thinned and Arjun could see the disapproval in her eyes. He didn't want her to get the wrong impression of his mother. "I'm going to tell you something that only my family knows." He swallowed to ease the lump in his throat, wondering why he wanted to share something so personal with Rani when he wasn't yet ready to tell her about Hema. "My biological mother died giving birth to me."

Rani gasped and squeezed his hand. "This is something I didn't know until recently," he continued. "My mother gave me so much love that not once did I question whether she was my real mother. My siblings who are her biological children still say I am my mother's favorite. She was heartbroken when I found out." So much so that his mother hadn't spoken to her own brother for years for telling Arjun.

"You would do anything for your mother, wouldn't you?"

Rani's voice held no judgment. Just soft understanding. Arjun nodded.

"Do you still think about Lakshmi?"

"Enough time has passed that I've let go." Or at least he did a good job pretending he had.

"It doesn't seem that way to me."

His heart stopped in his chest. On the pretense of taking the Thai food container, he extracted his hand from Rani's.

"So let's try this. I really miss street food."

"You're changing the subject."

He opened the lid of the container, and Rani passed him a fork. He chose his words carefully. "No one can take Lakshmi's place. She was my first love and you know what they say about first loves."

She nodded and a thought struck him. "Do you feel like you can never love someone the way you loved your ex?" The very idea of her confirming such an idea soured his mouth.

She took a bite of her food and chewed. He did the same, knowing that she needed time to formulate her answer, just as he needed a minute to prepare for it.

"I don't think I ever truly loved Navin. But he was the best among the choices I had. My parents expected me to marry an Indian and I wanted someone who understood what it's like to be an Indian American."

"And Navin was like that?"

"He was. But his family wasn't." She paused, clearly

weighing her words. "They were very traditional and it was hard for us to see eye to eye on a lot of things."

"Like?"

"They asked me to stop working because they didn't want people to think Navin didn't earn enough to support us. They were constantly harping on my weight. My mother-in-law would make me get on the scale to prove I was trying to lose weight. She would check the food in the kitchen to see what I'd eaten. They had access to Navin's bank accounts and constantly questioned the littlest purchases. It was suffocating."

Tears glittered in Rani's eyes and Arjun wanted desperately to get up and comfort her, but her story was hitting a little too close to home for him. His sisters' complaints echoed those of Rani.

"At first I resolved to work it out because I don't believe in divorce and Navin promised me that we'd only live with my in-laws for the first year so we could buy a big house of our own. As it turned out, his parents moved in with us when we did buy our house. And things were getting worse between me and Navin. He was constantly angry with me for every little thing— the way I hung my towel in the bathroom, if I sneezed too loudly, and on and on."

"I'm sorry, Rani."

She shrugged. "It's over now. I've learned my lesson— that you don't marry an Indian man, you marry his family. I wish I'd taken the time to get to know Navin's parents before I married him."

He nodded. That was one of the reasons why he had agreed to marry Hema. She was a family friend and familiar with the traditions of his house. He'd been in denial about the fact that he really had no choice in whom he could marry. Maybe that's why he hadn't told Rani about Hema. Telling Rani would make it a little too real, too inevitable for him.

He leaned forward. "Don't blame yourself, Rani. It was Navin's job to protect you from his parents."

She gave him a small smile. "It's very easy to say, but you know that's not how things work in Indian households. Navin would always remind me that I can walk away from him because I'm not blood but his parents will always be there for him. In the end I proved him right."

Arjun had no words. She may as well have been talking about his own parents. The *parampara* of his household were not just old fashioned, they were stringent. There weren't many intelligent, educated women who would be happy in such an atmosphere. But was it enough of a reason to marry Hema?

His assistant buzzed to let him know it was time for him to leave for a meeting. Rani stood and handed him the design folio she had arrived with. She held out her hand and he took it, holding onto it. "Rani, you are intelligent and beautiful, inside and out. Navin was a fool to let you go."

She gave him a brilliant smile and retracted her hand.

As he watched her leave, Arjun realized that Navin wasn't the only fool. He could no longer deny the fact that he was falling for her, and at the same time realized that there was no way they could be together.

# Eleven

As soon as Arjun opened the door, Rani could tell he was stressed. They had a rare evening off from work obligations and she'd just arrived at his condo so they could go out to dinner. His eyes were focused on her but had that faraway look like his mind was elsewhere.

He looked magazine-worthy in a perfectly cut black suit and an open-collared blue shirt. He kissed her lightly on the lips and her stomach fluttered. The more they were together, the hungrier she got for him. Part of her wanted to slow down on the hotel work and make him stay longer, and another part wanted to hurry up and get it done even faster. Ultimately, she had landed on the side of speed. The longer she spent with him, the harder it would be to give him up. They'd been together for three months now and she still couldn't get enough of him.

She'd resolved to talk to him today about how much longer he envisioned their affair lasting and what the terms of their breakup would be. While most of the work for his hotel would be completed in the next month, there would be follow-up items that could last for several months after he returned to India. She wanted to be prepared for the end, and to know with certainty when it was coming.

"We still have some time before dinner." He nuzzled her neck.

"How should we entertain ourselves?" she murmured as she untucked his shirt. She made quick work of the buttons then ran her hands over his abdomen, feeling the ripple of muscle and coarse line of hair that ran down the center of his belly and disappeared beneath his waistband. She popped the buttons on his pants and slid them down along with his boxer briefs. He was fully erect and she touched him, gently at first, then harder. She had never initiated sex before, always too unsure of herself to risk doing it wrong. But something had taken hold of her. Maybe it was the hungry way in which Arjun responded to her, mirroring the desire she felt for him. Or maybe it was the knowledge that their time together was winding down.

Whatever the case, she still couldn't believe how this sex symbol was enjoying what she was doing to him.

She had never gone down on a man before, had always felt it was awkward and a little on the disgusting side. But now, looking at Arjun's velvety skin, she wanted to drive him mad with pleasure, to be a seductress.

She knelt down and took him in her mouth. His low groan spurred her on until he stopped her. She looked at him. *Am I doing it wrong?*

"I want to come inside you, Rani," he said.

She wanted that too. She was strung tighter than a guitar wire. He moved to pick her up to take her to his bedroom, but she shook her head and directed him to sit on the couch. She lifted her dress, pushed down her panties and unhooked her bra. Navin would have looked at her naked body with disappointment. Arjun gazed at her with such feral hunger, it was easy to forget the past and focus on her fantasies.

She tore open a condom wrapper, sheathed him, and then straddled him, using her hand to guide him inside her. She rocked against him, focusing on the exact spots that pulsed inside her.

"Rani!" His voice was thick against her neck. "Slow it down."

She shook her head, unable to speak. She guided his hands towards her breasts. He squeezed them lightly. "Harder," she whispered urgently, rocking faster against him, taking him deeper inside.

Her body trembled as she climaxed. She always orgasmed with Arjun, but this time it was different. This was on her terms and she liked that. It was the first time she'd been in command of her pleasure. It was the most exhilarating and frightening experience of her life.

He pressed his forehead between her breasts. "Wow. When are you going to stop surprising me?"

She didn't answer him. Under the pretense of needing to use the bathroom, she took her leave so she could bring her quivering body under control. When she came out, he called for her to join him in his bedroom. Rani had been there a few times. Like the rest of the condo, it was minimally but comfortably furnished. There was a king-size platform bed with a navy velvet duvet. The side tables were gray and a white-and-gray rug accented the gray wood floor. It was a quintessential bachelor pad.

Arjun had already put his stylish Brioni suit back on. His shirt was miraculously wrinkle-free, though Rani suspected he had a closet full of them and this was just a fresh one.

"I want you to wear this dress for me."

He presented her with a black lace tea dress with a cowl back that dipped down low, leaving most of the back exposed. It was a stylishly retro dress by a designer that Rani could never afford. She'd spent a fortune on the dress she was wearing but apparently it didn't meet Arjun's expectations.

A familiar feeling of unease washed over her.

"It's beautiful, Arjun, but…"

He put a finger to her lips. "I saw it hanging in a shop window and couldn't stop thinking about how incredible it would look on you. I showed the saleswoman your picture and she guessed your size perfectly. Indulge me this once."

His phone rang and he stepped away. She eyed the dress, then slid it on. She had to admit it looked amazing on her, even if it wasn't her style. But something about accepting the dress didn't sit right. It reminded her of a time when she was in middle school and asked her mother if she could wear makeup. Her mother said no so Rani's friend suggested Rani use hers. Her skin itched but she wore the makeup anyway because she wanted so badly to fit in with the girls at school.

When Arjun returned, his gaze was so appreciative, Rani didn't have the heart to decline the dress. He took her to Joël Robuchon. Rani had never been there before; it was the only restaurant in Las Vegas that was so expensive that RKS staff had to get special permission before they could wine and dine clients there. The decor was 1930s French, with royal blue cushioned seats, thick, dark curtains and elaborate chandeliers. The wait staff were formally dressed and fell over themselves to show Arjun and Rani to a private room that could've held at least ten people. The head waiter explained that Arjun had reserved the entire room and ordered a sixteen-course tasting menu.

Rani gasped. "How will we eat that much food?"

He leaned over and whispered, "It's French. As my mother says, an Indian woman would be embarrassed to serve such small portions to dinner guests."

Rani laughed. Her mother would say something similar.

Before the meal even started, a waiter rolled out a bread cart with twenty different kinds of bread, served with hand-churned Normandy butter. Rani chose a saffron focaccia and Arjun took a rosemary brioche.

"I could be happy just with the breads on this cart." She buttered a piece and held it out to Arjun. He opened his mouth and sucked on the tips of her fingers as he took the bread. At her surprised gasp, he grinned. "Now I'm regretting the sixteen-course meal."

She pointed to the glass of wine the waiter had poured for her. Each course came with a wine pairing. "I'm actually looking forward to having a leisurely dinner where we can talk and enjoy each other's company."

"I think it's obvious how much I enjoy your company." His voice was low and seductive as he leaned over and brushed his lips across her earlobes.

Her nerves instantly tingled but she wasn't going to let him turn the conversation back to their sexual relationship.

"When I came to your condo, you looked very serious. Is everything okay?" she asked.

He sighed. "Solving everyone's problems in the family can be exhausting."

"Being the eldest is tiresome, isn't it?"

"What's it like for you?" he asked as the first course was served. The waiter described it in flourishing detail as a pan-seared foie gras with a grapefruit chardonnay reduction.

"It's different for me. My family is very middle class. My dad works in information technology and my mother is a schoolteacher. I don't have an empire to run. But I know what you mean about carrying the family burden. I thought my divorce was about my life and my happiness but my parents considered it to be a family decision. They haven't spoken to me in two years."

"Because of the divorce?"

She nodded. "It's bad enough that I divorced. It's even worse because I'm the eldest. They fear it'll reflect badly on the family and they'll have a harder time finding a *rishta* for my brother and sister."

"I know these things are important in India, but I

thought living in America, it wouldn't matter so much. Divorce is pretty common here. Most of the Indian Americans I meet are quite progressive."

She sighed. "My parents are ultra-traditional. They immigrated almost forty years ago but are still holding on to their customs hard and fast because giving even an inch means losing too much of themselves."

He nodded. "I understand only too well. My parents are the same. They've seen a lot of modernization, which is good for India, but they're having trouble accepting the social progress." He took a bite of the food and then a sip of his wine. "Do you keep in touch with your brother and sister?"

Rani nodded. "We're pretty close. And ironically, as much as my parents worry that I've sullied our name and no one will want to marry into our family, neither one of my siblings will accept something as archaic as an arranged marriage."

Was it her imagination or did the wineglass in Arjun's hand tremble ever so slightly?

"There are some good reasons to have your marriage arranged."

Rani looked at him, an uneasy feeling creeping deep into her belly. "Like what?"

He swallowed. "Like knowing that two people share the same family values and expectations."

Rani stopped midchew. Why did Arjun sound like he wasn't just talking hypothetically?

"Would you accept an arranged marriage?"

"I already have."

Rani dropped her fork and it clanked loudly as it hit

her plate. She must not have heard him correctly. "Excuse me, what?"

"There's an arrangement between my family and good friends that I'll marry their daughter Hema."

Rani's heart dropped to her toes. *I'm not hearing this right.* "You've been cheating on your fiancée with me?"

Her stomach roiled and for a minute she thought the delicious food she'd just eaten would come back up.

"Hema and I aren't engaged. She knows I date, and so does she. Our families went into business together five years ago and our parents want to solidify our relationship with a marriage. Eventually."

"And you didn't think to tell me this before?"

"I didn't think it mattered. We decided early on that this is a temporary affair."

Rage boiled through her veins. "Excuse me, I decide what matters to me. I don't sleep with another woman's man."

"Rani, Hema and I are not together in the traditional sense. We've never been physical with each other. If I had to characterize our relationship, I would say she's like a family member, almost like my sister. Our impending marriage is an obligation. One that I only agreed to because after what happened with Lakshmi, I'll never fall in love with anyone again."

Rani tried to ignore the searing pain that cut through her heart. He had made a part of her blossom that she'd never thought existed, given her a new sexual confidence. She'd hoped she had opened his heart enough to believe that he could love again.

The waiter placed a second course before them with some fanfare. At another time Rani would have admired the artfully presented charcuterie but she was quaking with anger.

Arjun tried to take her hand but she snatched it away.

"How dare you keep something like this from me."

"It is not relevant to our relationship."

"You don't get to decide that for us! Am I just a roll in the hay for you? A sex partner?"

"Rani, I've come to care for you. More than I've cared for anyone since Lakshmi. It was not my intention to deceive you. The arrangement with Hema is not mine to share. Her parents invested a billion dollars in a partnership with me to expand our hotel chain globally. While my company is privately held, Hema's family business is traded on the Bombay Stock Exchange. We have to carefully control our wedding announcement. Even an accidental slip to the media could have repercussions. No one outside my immediate family knows about it. It's not something we discuss with outsiders."

*An outsider. That's how he thinks of me.*

Rani speared whatever was on her plate and stuck it in her mouth to keep from screaming.

"Say something, Rani."

She cleared her throat. "I need to use the restroom." She needed to get away from him. To have a minute to regain her composure.

In the bathroom she stood in front of the mirror and splashed cold water on her wrists. Her stomach twisted into a thousand knots.

*What did I expect? He's an Indian man who thinks he knows best.*

She'd been a fool to think she was sophisticated enough to have an affair with a man like Arjun and come away unscathed. To think herself capable of separating the physical from the emotional. What had she been expecting? That he'd fall in love with her? And then what? Forsake his family and live with her in Vegas? She wasn't about to move to India and play the dutiful wife and daughter-in-law. There was no scenario where she and Arjun would have a happily-ever-after.

So why was she upset? This wasn't news to her. She'd wanted to talk to him about when their affair would end. Now that she knew about Hema, she had her answer. It was best to end it now before someone got hurt.

"Rani?" She looked up to see Delia come out of one of the stalls. Could this dinner get any worse?

"What are you doing here?" Rani flinched at the high pitch in her voice.

"Mr. Rabat and I are here with a client we're courting," Delia replied evenly, looking Rani over. "Are you here on a date?"

Rani shook her head. There was a good chance they'd see her with Arjun. "I'm here with Mr. Singh."

Delia lifted a brow. "I don't remember giving approval to dine him here."

"He invited me," she said, her throat dry.

"Well that certainly explains the dress."

"Excuse me?" The dress might be a touch revealing but it wasn't that risqué.

"I'm no fashionista but that has to be couture. Is it a gift from a certain wealthy client?"

Rani's cheeks burned. "Is your dinner going well?" she asked, trying to change the subject as Delia washed her hands.

"I think so. But it's not as big a contract as you got

out of Mr. Singh. Quite an accomplishment. I see you're working hard at it." She gave Rani a thin smile in the mirror, then straightened and dried her hands. "Enjoy your dinner."

As Delia breezed out of the room, Rani leaned on the sink. She wanted to hate Delia but she couldn't blame her. Everyone would see it the way Delia obviously had: that Rani had slept with Arjun to get the contract. While her job might be safe, once again her talent would be overshadowed by rumor and innuendo. *And for what? Some good sex with a hottie? Okay, mind-blowing sex with a damn hot hottie.* But what would come of it? He would leave and marry someone else and she'd be left with her heart in tatters and a reputation to repair.

*8>He stops at nothing to get his way.*

She squared her shoulders. There was only one thing left to do.

Arjun tried not to look at his phone to see how long Rani had been gone. It felt like forever. She seemed really upset about Hema. Maybe Rani was getting too attached. He never started an affair without an end date in mind and would cut things off even earlier if he sensed that they were getting tired of each other. With Rani, he figured the hotel opening would be their last night together. They wouldn't be working together anymore and he'd be returning to India. But he was more bothered by her behavior than he should be. He had gotten too close to Rani. Their affair had crossed the boundaries he normally set for himself.

When she returned to the table, he didn't like the expression on her face.

"I insisted that we get a few courses at one time. I'm pretty sure the chef is so appalled that he'll never let me back into this restaurant again." He kept his tone lighthearted.

Rani took her seat. He reached out for her hand but she busied herself placing her napkin on her lap.

"What's wrong, Rani?"

She sighed. "I'm wondering how long you'd planned for our affair to continue."

The question caught him off guard. "Why do we need a specific date? I have been enjoying what we have. We can continue for as long as we are both liking each other's company."

*What am I saying? Am I really going to continue on with Rani when I get back to India?* He usually knew his mind, and didn't give in to temptation. So why couldn't he just tell Rani what he had planned for them?

"What about when the hotel is finished?"

"I'll go back to India but I will be coming back to Vegas to check on things. And I have a great owners condo that'll feel just like home." He gave her his best smile.

"So, what, you want to continue this indefinitely?"

*No, I don't.* He knew what she was asking and he was prepared with a response. So why was he hesitating? The answer became clear to him as she looked up at him with shining eyes.

"I don't know, Rani. Obviously it cannot be forever. I'm going to marry Hema and I'm not a cheater. That wouldn't be fair to you or her."

"Now you're thinking of Hema? You didn't consider her when we first got together? Or of how I'd feel about her?"

"I've told you, Hema and I are just friends right now. She knows I sleep with other women."

Rani blanched. "I can't do this anymore, Arjun."

"Do what exactly? Have dinner with me? Sleep with me? Work with me?" Why was his voice so sharp?

A tear threatened to escape the corner of her eye and he longed to touch her, but she scraped her chair back and stood.

"I think you and I both know that we can't continue this affair."

And with that, she walked out. He wanted to go after her, at least drop her back at her place, but his feet seemed nailed to the floor.

Because it was best to let her go.

# Twelve

*I'm okay, I really am.*

It had been two weeks since Rani's ill-fated dinner with Arjun. They had managed to avoid each other as she threw herself into working feverishly to get his hotel finished. Contractors were already finalizing the guest suites, a feat that had been accomplished by Arjun offering a hefty bonus for early completion. But there was no avoiding him at this afternoon's meeting at the hotel to review the progress that had been made. She had most of her team attending to serve as a buffer between them.

"Rani, I need to talk to you." Delia shut the door as she entered her office.

Rani took a deep breath.

"I talked with Mr. Rabat and he's in agreement that I will run the meeting this afternoon with Mr. Singh."

"Excuse me? This is my project."

"Given your personal involvement with Mr. Singh, we don't think you should continue as the project lead."

"There is nothing going on between me and Mr. Singh." It was technically true. She had purposely used the present tense.

"But something did happen."

Rani closed her eyes and took a deep breath. Maybe she should let Delia take over the entire project. Then Rani wouldn't have to see Arjun again.

*No. Damn it.* She had an ace up her sleeve. She could throw Delia's hypocrisy in her face by reminding her that she was Rani's boss because of her own personal relationship. But she wasn't going to stoop to her level.

"We don't want to be late. You want to run the meeting, fine. I hope you've walked the space, cataloged the progress and talked to all the contractors so you're prepared." She walked out the door, leaving Delia no choice but to follow.

When Rani got to the hotel, she saw that Arjun had armed himself with an entourage. The smells of paint, dust and cut wood filled the air. Delia led the tour, but Rani constantly interjected, pointing out the areas where they were ahead of schedule and the ways in which they had incorporated unique architectural details. Just a few months ago, Rani wouldn't have dared to act so brazenly, but she was tired of everybody making decisions for her. Maybe Arjun had rubbed off on her. It was her project and Delia had no right to take it over.

Arjun stayed toward the back of the group. When

the tour was done, they gathered in the newly finished lobby. "Any questions?" Delia asked crisply.

"Yes." The sea of staff parted so Rani had a complete view of Arjun. Her chest tightened, making it hard for her to take the breath she desperately needed. He was wearing jeans and a polo shirt. He'd come casual today as they'd been asked to do; they were all required to wear hard hats and there was no avoiding getting dusty. She loved how he looked in jeans and there was no stopping her mind from picturing the muscular legs underneath the fabric.

"Yes, Mr. Singh?"

Arjun had a number of technical questions, none of which Delia could answer, so Rani answered them for her.

"I have a final question," Arjun persisted. "Why are you running this meeting when Ms. Gupta has all the answers?"

Rani wanted to kiss him.

"I'll be leading the project from this point forward," Delia stated matter-of-factly.

Rani's head snapped towards Delia. *What? How dare she!*

"That is unacceptable," Arjun said simply. "Ms. Gupta has done a tremendous job and I prefer to work with her."

Rani froze and so did every member of the RKS team. Mr. Rabat was also there, eager to make sure everything went well because Arjun had managed to negotiate an unusual clause in the contract that allowed him to fire the firm with little notice.

With courage she didn't know she had, Rani calmly

said, "We felt you might want a more senior member of the team at this critical juncture, but you are the client and RKS wants you to be happy." She looked smugly at Mr. Rabat, who reluctantly nodded.

After everyone had left, Rani felt drained but there was one more thing she wanted to do. She walked into the owners condo, which hadn't been toured or discussed today because they'd already been signed off on. As she did, her phone buzzed with two missed calls from her brother, Sohel. She dialed his number but he didn't answer.

Her feet carried her into the master bedroom. The place where she'd made love to Arjun for the first time. She touched the bedspread, her body warming at the memory of the textured fabric on her naked back. And the warmth of Arjun's body on top of hers.

"What are you doing here?"

Rani whirled, her phone falling from her hands as she did.

"I'm sorry, I didn't mean to startle you." Arjun stood there looking at her with a pained expression on his face.

"I...I just wanted to... I... Sorry. I'll leave." She felt like a trespasser. She picked up her phone and moved past him but he caught her hand. She stopped, hating the way she liked the warm feeling of his touch.

"Mr. Singh, I don't think this is professional."

He let her go. "Fine, then. I'll tell you why I came. I couldn't stop thinking about our night here. About how good it felt to be with you, how right we were together. I came back to convince myself that you meant nothing to me."

A strangled sound escaped her throat but before she could say more, her phone vibrated. She glanced at the screen. It was her brother, Sohel, again.

"I'm sorry, I need to take this."

"I don't like how we ended things, Rani. We need to talk."

That was the last thing Rani wanted to do. He would tempt her back into his bed and she couldn't do that. It wasn't just that he was promised to someone. It was the fact that he hadn't told her. He'd made the decision about what she needed to know. He'd been controlling their relationship right from the start, and she'd let him. Just like she'd let everyone around her walk all over her for her whole life.

The phone buzzed incessantly in her hand. Arjun sighed in frustration as she answered it and walked into the hallway.

Her brother didn't waste time with pleasantries. As soon as she heard what he said, her stomach bottomed out.

"Oh my God. No! I'll be there as soon as I can."

"Is everything okay?" Arjun asked as soon as she stabbed the End button.

She shook her head, unable to stop the tears burning her eyes. He came to her and pulled her into his arms. She collapsed against him, hating herself for needing his strength. "That was my brother. My father had a stroke. He's critical." She choked on a sob. "He might not make it through the night. Sohel asked me to come immediately to say goodbye."

She pushed against Arjun and tapped her phone. "I need to find a flight to Los Angeles."

Rani called the travel agency that RKS used. Even after explaining the situation, the best the travel agent could do was put her on a standby flight; she would have to wait hours to get a seat. Rani cursed in frustration, bile rising in her throat. What if her father died before she could see him? She shook her head; she couldn't think that way. She had to find a way to get to Los Angeles.

Arjun gently took the phone away from her and ended the call.

"Arjun no. I have to…"

"Rani, I have a flight for you."

She looked at him wide-eyed.

"I have a membership with an aviation company. They'll have a private plane ready for us at Henderson Executive Airport in thirty minutes. Henderson is a lot less busy at this time than McCarran so we can get underway faster."

She sagged in relief and then it hit her. *"We?"* Her voice was a squeak.

"Yes. I'm not letting you deal with this alone. I'll fly you there."

"You don't have to do that. I appreciate your help in getting me a flight. I'll pay you back."

He shook his head. "Whatever else we are or are not, I insist that we are friends and I will see you safely to LA. It's only a little more than an hour's flight." He firmly led her out. "Let's get going."

As much as she wanted to resist, the words of protest didn't come out. There were so many emotions wreaking havoc with her, she didn't have the energy to think about why Arjun was coming with her.

"I'll have one of my assistants retrieve your car and drive it to your house."

She nodded, glad that he was calm enough to think through the logistical details.

A Cessna Citation XLS was waiting for them when they arrived at the small airport. Rani had never been here. Then again, she'd never flown in a private plane.

They wasted no time climbing into the cabin. There were seats along both sides of the plane, facing each other, eight in total, clad in luxurious cream leather. Arjun took the seat opposite Rani and buckled in. Rani noticed a refrigerator that contained refreshments.

The pilot greeted them and went over safety instructions, and then they were on their way.

"Sorry this plane is a little basic. I have a Gulfstream back in India but it was impractical to station it here for the few trips I take in the US"

She looked at him incredulously. "Are you kidding me? I was going to spend most of the night at the airport getting bumped from one standby flight to another and then cram myself into a middle seat that's only comfortable for a small child. This is not basic. This is luxury that common people like me only read about in books or hear about from wealthy clients like you."

He winced and Rani regretted her tone. "Do you have any updates on your father?" he asked, changing the subject.

She shook her head. "I just texted Sohel to let him know that I'm on my way. He's in the ICU. He hasn't told my mom that I'm coming. He thinks it's best that I just show up."

"Do you think your parents will refuse to see you, even now?"

The tears she'd been holding back spilled onto her cheeks. She turned her face away from him. "I don't know. The very fact that Sohel isn't telling my mother that I'm on the way to the hospital means he doesn't think she'll see me." Rani remembered the last time she'd shown up at her childhood home. Her parents had refused to open the door. They'd left her knocking, and then sitting on the porch for hours.

Arjun reached out and touched her hand, which was resting on her lap. "When I was little, there was a time that I broke this crystal statue that Ma kept on her dresser. It was her favorite—she told me many times that it was a special present from my grandfather who had died a few years before. I was forbidden from touching it, but of course I was curious, and one day I broke it while playing with it. She was so angry. She told me to leave her room and wouldn't talk to me for the rest of the day. I was so upset and inconsolable. I was sure she didn't love me anymore. But then she came to tuck me into bed, like she did every night, and told me that no matter what I do, or how I hurt her, she would always love me. You have to believe that your parents are the same way, Rani. They may be unable to see past their anger right now but they love you, and always will."

She nodded through her tears but then the sobs took over her body, and the grief she had bottled away came pouring out. He unbuckled his seat belt, went to her side and pulled her into his arms, holding on to her as she clung to him.

* * *

When they reached Los Angeles, they took the private car Arjun had already arranged for them to Cedars-Sinai hospital. They found Sohel and Rani's sister Anaya in the ICU waiting room. The siblings hugged for several minutes, crying into each other's shoulders.

Rani's brother was nearly six feet tall. He was dressed in a black T-shirt and jeans and his thick hair was unruly. Anaya was a petite version of Rani, barely five feet tall. She had glossy black hair pulled back into a ponytail and big dark eyes. She was similarly dressed in jeans and a T-shirt.

Arjun stepped away from them, not wanting to intrude on the family moment, and he didn't want to put Rani in an awkward position by having to explain his presence.

"What are you doing here?"

They all turned when they heard the harsh question. Arjun guessed that the woman in the *salwar kameez*—the traditional Indian pants with a long tunic top, and a scarf called a *dupatta* covering her head—was Rani's mother. He could see the family resemblance.

"Mum!" Rani stepped towards her mother, who held up her hand.

"You should not be here, Rani. Your father is in no condition to deal with you. Please, go away."

Rani shrank back. The look of sheer pain on her face propelled Arjun forward to make sure she didn't collapse. Her mother eyed him.

"Namaste, Auntie." He joined his hands together in front of him and bowed his head in a sign of respect. He could have called her Mrs. Gupta rather than using the more intimate, common term for older women in India. But this would identify him as a friend rather than as an outsider.

Mrs. Gupta appraised him. "And who are you?"

"Arjun Singh. I'm Rani's...colleague."

Her eyes widened and she looked between Arjun and Rani. "I see," she said wearily and sat down in a chair.

Rani sat beside her and clasped her mother's hand. "Mum, what good will come of sending me away again? Please, I'm begging you, I don't want to leave Dad like this."

Her mother closed her eyes and put her head in her hands. Before she could say anything, a man dressed in scrubs appeared.

"Mrs. Gupta?"

The entire family stood, dread written on their faces.

The man turned to Mrs. Gupta. "I'm Dr. McNeil, the neurologist who's been taking care of your husband since he arrived. I have an update."

Mrs. Gupta placed a hand on her chest.

"You were very wise in bringing Mr. Gupta right after his symptoms began. We were able to give him medication that only works if you administer it within three hours, and ideally within the hour after a stroke. Early tests show that he's responding well. He's awake now, which is a really good sign. You can go see him, but please keep it short."

They all breathed a collective sigh of relief.

Rani rose, but one look from her mother had her collapsing back in the chair. Mrs. Gupta, Sohel and Anaya followed the doctor through the ICU doors.

Rani sobbed into her hands. Arjun sat next to her

and put an arm around her. She rested her head on his shoulder. "What will it take for them to forgive me? I did everything I could to work it out with Navin. I really did."

"Just be here, Rani. Be here for your parents. Even if they don't want you around, show them that you haven't forsaken them. That you are here for them. Eventually they will remember their love."

"I don't think they'll ever forgive me. Today is the test. If my father still refuses to see me then I really am dead to them."

"When I told my mother that I loved Lakshmi and was going to marry her despite what they said, she threatened to disown me. And she meant it too. She didn't speak to me, had the servants pack my bags and wouldn't let me in the house. I had to go stay in the guest cottage. Even after things ended with Lakshmi, she wouldn't talk to me, not even to say I told you so. I understand how you're feeling. Like a piece of your heart has been cut out from your chest and you're left to bleed on the street. But I showed up to ask my mother's forgiveness every day for a month. And I didn't stop until she finally let me in the door. She did not talk to me for another two months but eventually she did. There will come a point when your parents will also realize they are not as angry as they want to be."

"That's good advice," said a voice from behind them. They both turned to see Sohel, who was smiling. "Dad wants to see you, Rani. When he opened his eyes and saw all of us standing there his first question was to ask where you were."

Rani stood so fast that she nearly tripped. Arjun steadied her, then she followed Sohel into the ICU.

Arjun smiled, relief flooding through him. Rani's anguish had torn him apart. He knew what it felt like to make a choice that hurt the people he cared about. He had felt so selfish for wanting Lakshmi at the expense of his family. At the time he was young, and nothing felt more important, but could he make the same choice now?

Rani was not just an affair, that much he had come to understand in the last few weeks. No matter how many times he went over the reasons they couldn't be together, all he could think about was how much he missed her. He'd been so happy to see her at the hotel walk-through that he'd spent the entire meeting thinking of frivolous excuses to extend the work on the hotel so he'd have more time in Vegas. More time with her.

He rubbed his forehead with the tips of his fingers. There had to be a way for the two of them to be together. He was a good problem solver so why couldn't he solve this one?

*Because there is no reasoning with Ma.* He loved his mother but emotion and tradition were a big part of how she made decisions. Did that emotion also apply to forgiving her son? She had eventually forgiven him for falling in love with Lakshmi, hadn't she?

The answer was no. Their relationship had never been the same after that. Where before there had been implicit trust, after the affair with Lakshmi his mother needed constant validations that he would follow through on basic promises. *You're sure you'll come to the party? When exactly will you talk to your sister about that problem?*

And of course the big one: *You promise you'll marry Hema the second you return from Vegas?*

# Thirteen

Fifteen minutes later, Arjun didn't have any answers as Rani came out of the ICU doors with tears in her eyes. He stood and went to her side, putting his arms around her, and she sobbed against his chest. "He still hasn't forgiven me."

Arjun's heart sank. How heartless could Rani's father be? Surely facing mortality would have softened him just a little.

Rani folded herself into the waiting room chair. Arjun sat next to her and put a protective arm around her. Sohel and Anaya joined them a few minutes later.

"Excuse me." Arjun turned to see Anaya eyeing him shyly. "Are you *the* Arjun Singh? India's hottest hottie?"

Rani stiffened. He looked down to see a small smile tug at her lips. Then she touched her hand to her forehead in a face-palm. Anaya's voice was so teenage fangirl that in this austere environment, it broke the tension.

He smiled and nodded. "That's me."

Anaya clapped a hand to her mouth. "I knew it. I didn't want to say anything before but I just knew it was you." She pulled out her phone and swiped. "Do you mind taking a selfie with me? My friends at school will be sooooooo jealous."

The slight shake of Rani's shoulders and the amused expression on her face were well worth the ten pictures Anaya proceeded to take, stopping in the middle to put on lipstick and change locations because the light wasn't hitting her right.

"You should get going," Rani told Arjun.

He shook his head. "I'm not leaving you, Rani."

"But you must have a million things to deal with."

He took Rani's hand and squeezed it. "None of that is important. The only thing that matters to me right now is taking care of you."

Her eyes glistened. "Don't do this, Arjun," she whispered. His heart dropped into this stomach. Were they so far gone that he didn't have the right to see her through something so difficult?

In the end, Arjun prevailed. They spent the night in the hospital. Sohel and Anaya curled up on the waiting room chairs. Rani let her head drop onto Arjun's shoulder and dozed off. They woke early the next day as the morning shift arrived at the hospital.

"Why don't I get you guys some coffee and breakfast," Arjun volunteered. He found the hospital cafeteria and bought food for everyone. When he returned to the waiting room, Rani's mother was there too. They were all sitting in a circle with their heads bowed. At first Arjun feared the worst, but then he realized they were praying. His mother had done enough *pujas* for him to recognize that the Sanskrit prayer they were uttering was one of thanks, not of mourning.

He stood a few feet away. It was one thing for him to have been here yesterday when Rani first arrived, but his presence this morning would raise uncomfortable questions with her mother. He knew how an Indian parent would perceive their "friendship."

Anaya looked up and saw him first. She rushed over to help him with the two cafeteria trays he carried laden with food and drinks. "You won't believe it. Dad's doing much better. The doctor's just told *Amma* that he's taken a turn for the better. BTW, what should I call you?"

"That's great news, Anaya, and you can call me Arjun."

They all thanked Arjun for the food and dug in, their spirits clearly resorted.

"Arjun, in what capacity are you here?" Rani stiffened at her mother's question, and Arjun's pulse quickened.

"They are in love, *Amma*," Anaya bubbled.

"Anaya!" Rani called out sharply.

"Oh, don't try to hide it. I heard you guys talking. He said you were the most important thing to him and he was going to take care of you. You're in looooove with India's hottest hottie," her sister said in a singsong voice.

Arjun's mouth went dry. He was normally so vigilant about appearances. Why hadn't he been more careful around Anaya?

"Anaya, stop it." Rani said in a high-pitched voice. "We are colleagues, that's all."

Arjun caught Mrs. Gupta's eyes and his heart sank. She was looking at him appraisingly. It was a look he was very familiar with, one that Indian aunties with eligible daughters often gave him. He wanted to say something, to correct Anaya, but his tongue was stuck in his mouth. Anything he said would make things worse for Rani. He needed to let her handle it.

"Rani, why don't you tell us what your relationship is to Arjun," her mother said quietly.

Rani gave him a stricken look. "We're friends, *Amma*. Yesterday when I heard about Dad, Arjun helped me get a flight here."

"Did you come on a private plane?" Anaya asked eagerly, totally oblivious to Rani's discomfort.

"A very small one," Arjun replied. Hoping to give Rani some time to think, he went on to describe the aircraft, which led to questions about the one he owned in India. He took his time talking about that one, as well. He'd hoped once they'd exhausted the subject, the conversation would steer toward a topic other than their relationship, but Rani's mother was not to be deterred.

"You must be very good friends for Arjun to help you like that. I'm guessing you're a very busy man, yet here you are bringing us food and keeping Rani company."

Rani looked down, fidgeting with her purse.

"Rani, it would ease your father's mind to know that you are engaged to someone else. Especially someone as suitable as Arjun." Rani's mother gave her a hard look.

Rani shrank in her chair and looked at Arjun in

alarm. "We're not getting engaged, Mum," she finally said, her voice leaden.

Her mother looked between Rani and Arjun then sighed. "After you left yesterday, your father was so upset. Every time he sees you, all he can think about is how you've ruined your life." Rani opened her mouth to say something but her mother raised her hand sternly. Mrs. Gupta would get along really with his own mother. She had a way of making everyone feel like they were still little children being scolded for having dirty hands.

"It will make him so happy to know that you have found a way to be happy again. With one decision, Rani, one announcement, you can erase everything that's happened in the past and focus on the future."

Tears streamed down Rani's face and Arjun's chest hurt. She was in so much pain and he couldn't bear it. "It's not my decision to make, Mum." Her voice was small and very quiet, as if she had no breath left in her body.

"Rani's right, Auntie, the decision is not hers, it's mine." Arjun said. *What am I saying?* The right course of action here would be to explain that they were just friends, which was technically true of their current relationship status, and then extricate himself from the situation.

Instead, he couldn't believe what came out of his mouth next.

"The time is not right, but I think it would be best if I talk to you and Uncle privately so I can ask for Rani's hand in marriage."

Rani's eyes widened. Anaya squealed and clapped, and Mrs. Gupta wiped her eyes with the end of her *dupatta*. "Bless you, my son. This news will have Rani's dad out of this hospital in no time." She stood and hugged Arjun while Rani stared at him openmouthed.

*What have I done?*

# Fourteen

*How dare he!* Everything was happening so fast that Rani couldn't process the flood of emotions drowning her, but the one bubbling through her body was anger. He had no right to interfere with her family, especially without consulting her. Has he forgotten that he's scheduled to marry another woman?

"I'm going to ask if your father can have visitors." As soon as Rani's mother left, Rani pulled Arjun into the corner, out of earshot of her siblings.

"What the hell did you just do?" she snarled.

He placed his hands on her shoulders. "I couldn't stand to see you hurt like that, Rani. I have a solution. I'll tell your dad that I want to marry you. He will forgive you and you can finally reunite with your family."

"Are you kidding me? How dare you think you can

be my savior? What's going to happen when they realize we lied to them? They'll hate me for the rest of my life. You had no right to get involved. This is my situation. I'll handle it!"

"There you are. The doctor says we can go right in." Rani's mother was back, grabbing Arjun's hand and pulling him towards the ICU doors.

Rani followed hurriedly behind him. "*Amma*, I don't think this is the right time to be discussing all this with Dad. Let him come home and then I'll explain everything."

Rani's mother had already pressed the doorbell requesting access to the ICU, and the large double doors swung open. "Don't be silly, Rani. There is no time like the present. Your father will be so happy."

"No, *Amma*, you're not listening…"

"Rani, I know what's best for you." With that her mother went barreling down the hallway towards her father's bed. She looked at Arjun, who squeezed her arm. "It'll be fine, Rani, trust me," he said softly.

Her mother turned and gave an impatient wave for them to follow.

Rani stood there feeling like she was fourteen years old again, being told by her mother that dating was for American girls. Rani would be a good Indian daughter and marry one of the men her parents introduced her to after she graduated college. *Trust me, Rani, I know what's best for you,* her mother had said.

Her father's room had clear glass doors. The incessant beeps of medical machines assaulted them as they entered. Bright white lights cast an unnatural pallor on all their faces.

Rani stepped towards her father's bed but her mother stopped her, pushing Arjun towards him instead. Rani needed to stop this. But even as she formulated the words, she knew it was too late.

As Arjun began speaking to her father, a hysterical laugh bubbled inside Rani but she stifled it. Most American men would introduce themselves first but Arjun started by presenting his family history, listing the members of his current family, then detailing his family business, alluding to but not outright proclaiming his wealth. And *then* he talked about himself. It was exactly what her parents expected, and by the adoring looks they gave Arjun, they were already smitten.

The beaming smile on her father's face should have brought her joy, but her heart sank to her toes. From her parents' perspective, Arjun was a catch. He came from a good family, was wealthy, cultured and traditional.

The words her mother didn't say in the waiting room didn't escape Rani: that Arjun would erase Navin from their lives. When her parents talked about her, they wouldn't have to explain that she was divorced and answer the inevitable string of questions that followed. Navin's family had spared no hatred in portraying Rani as a spoiled, Westernized woman who left the marriage because she didn't want to give her in-laws the respect they deserved. *Must be her upbringing, her parents didn't teach her right.* But if she remarried, the community would no longer point fingers.

"Rani, you have made me so happy. Come here." With heavy feet, she stepped towards her father's bedside and leaned down to give him a hug. It had been three years since he'd held her. The last time was when she'd come home crying, her packed bags in the car. She'd sobbed her troubles to her parents and they'd listened, her father holding her and letting her smear her makeup into his shirt. But then they'd told her to go back to her marital home. To find a way to work it out with Navin and her in-laws. *In a marriage, you must sacrifice yourself, Rani. Learn to suffer, they'd said.*

"When will the wedding be?" Rani's mother asked.

Rani opened her mouth to say there would be no wedding but her throat was too tight. Her father looked so happy; there was even some color in his face.

"I'm not sure yet, Auntie," Arjun said evenly. "I have to finish my hotel in Vegas, and then of course I will have to take Rani to India to meet my parents, and we can make decisions after that."

Her mother pursed her lips but said nothing. Arjun had that way about him, of respectfully brooking no argument. He was used to taking charge; in fact, just like her parents before him, he'd taken charge of her life.

"Well don't wait too long, I'm sure you'll be wanting children." The response came from her father and Rani reddened.

"Your family is so traditional. How do they feel about Rani being divorced?" her mother asked.

Rani closed her eyes and sighed. Being divorced did not make her a damaged commodity but as she'd told herself countless times, her parents had grown up in a different generation, at a time when being divorced was a character flaw.

"I don't have a problem with Rani being divorced. From what she's told me, it sounds like it was a terrible situation and I'm glad she got herself out. She's an amazing woman and her ex-husband was a fool to let her go."

Rani softened a little at Arjun's words. Her mother nodded as if she agreed with him but Rani knew it was a nod of relief.

"My parents don't know I want to marry Rani, which is why we need to wait until Rani and I can travel to India so that I can have the opportunity to tell them in person and explain the situation."

How would his parents react? Rani had never allowed herself to think about the fact that even if he refused to marry Hema, his parents might not accept a divorced woman for Arjun.

*What am I thinking? All this isn't real! He's still going to marry Hema. This is all an act.* One that Arjun had planned without consulting her. He would go back to India and leave her with a big mess to clean up.

"What if they don't accept?" Rani's father asked.

"We will cross that bridge when we come to it," Arjun said diplomatically. "What's important now is that Uncle gets better."

"We'll need to celebrate. As soon as you are out of the hospital, we should throw a dinner party at our house," Rani's mother gushed.

Arjun shook his head. "Let's not get ahead of ourselves. Once Uncle is well, Rani and I will need to rush back to Vegas to finish the hotel."

Her mother nodded. "Yes, the sooner you finish that hotel, the faster you can go back to India and firm things up with your parents."

And then it struck Rani. That was Arjun's ticket out. He would say that his parents didn't agree. For now she was back in her parents' fold, and when he dumped her later on, it wouldn't technically be her fault. Her stomach bottomed out.

"We should go and let Dad rest," she said, desperate to get out of there before things got worse. She would make Arjun leave tonight and tell her parents he had an emergency at the hotel. The less time her parents spent with Arjun, the better. She didn't need them falling in love with him too.

When they stepped outside, Sohel and Anaya were eager to know how things went. Rani brushed past them and ushered Arjun into the hallway to the elevators. She had to get away from her family. When they got to the lobby, she spotted a sign for the hospital gardens and dragged him outside with her.

The garden consisted of a courtyard with some flowering plants and metal picnic tables. It was relatively empty save for a few patients nursing cups of coffee and eating off cafeteria trays.

She didn't bother sitting down; her entire body was shaking with anger. "What were you thinking? Do you know what'll happen when our fake engagement breaks up? My parents will blame me again. They'll point out how my past has come back to haunt me and how I'll never have happiness. You'll play right into their beliefs that a divorce is a lifelong sentence for loneliness."

She was flailing her arms, her emotions raw and uncontrolled. The stress of the last few days had unraveled her.

Arjun captured her hands in his and pulled her close. "Rani, why do you think this is all fake?"

Her heart slammed into her ribs. *Wait, what?*

She stared at him, her throat tight.

"The last few weeks without you have been hell on me. I'm in love with you, Rani, and I don't want to be without you. I wasn't lying to your parents. I want us to be together."

She had to be hallucinating. The stress had finally gotten to her and she was about to crack. There was no other explanation for the words she was hearing from Arjun's mouth.

"What about Hema?"

"I agreed to marry Hema because it was good for business. Hema doesn't want to marry me. She's doing it out of obligation."

"What about your parents?"

"It will not be easy. None of this will be easy. For me or for you. But right now we don't have to think about all that. All I need to know is that you love me, and that you want to be with me. Everything else, we can figure out."

*He loves me.* There were a thousand *but*s that went through her head. *But* what about his family? *But* how would they work it out? *But* what about what she wanted?

"You know I make my own decisions. I don't like how you took charge of the situation with my parents. I won't be controlled, Arjun."

"That's why I love you, Rani. You are your own woman. I should have talked to you before I said something to your parents. I just couldn't stand to see you in so much pain."

Arjun pulled her into his arms and she savored the strength of his body, the beating of his heart. Its rhythm matched her own. She'd been herself with him. Never pretended to be someone she wasn't. And he still wanted her.

"Do you love me, Rani?" he whispered into her ear.

*That's not the right question. The question is whether I can love you, whether I'm strong enough to love you.*

"I've fought with myself. I haven't wanted to, but I've fallen in love with you."

He kissed her then. A soul-searing kiss that left no doubt in her heart about how she felt about him.

Neither of them noticed Anaya snapping their picture.

# Fifteen

Arjun had to return to Las Vegas, but Rani remained behind until her father was released a few days later. He'd made a speedy recovery, but the specialist warned the family that he was still fragile and at high risk for another stroke.

Once he got home, Rani's parents insisted she stay, and she drank in the love of her family. Sohel had his own condo on the other side of town but he stayed in his old bedroom too. It was just like it had been growing up, with all of them together under one roof.

Anaya, Sohel and Rani were sitting on the brown-and-yellow shag rug in the family basement playing *Monopoly*. The room looked like it was stuck in the '70s, with a nut-brown couch that almost blended into the rug. The walls were covered in green-and-yellow wallpaper. It was an obnoxiously decorated room but it comforted Rani like a ratty stuffed bear. There were many childhood memories here: watching Bollywood movies with the family, laughing at vacation pictures and sleeping together on thin mattresses when the cousins came to visit from India. Her parents never had much in terms of money but they gave their children every spare minute of time they had.

"You've cut your hair so short." Rani's mother sat on the couch behind Rani and began braiding her daughter's loose hair. Rani savored the feeling of her mother's hands on her scalp. When she was a child, her mother braided her hair every morning before she left for school. At the time Rani complained and promptly undid the braids when she left the house because the kids made fun of her.

She'd only appreciated how much her mother had sacrificed when she'd had to watch Navin's two nieces for a week one summer. Rani had still been working and her mother-in-law had purposefully assigned Rani to take care of the two girls to prove to Rani that she couldn't work and take care of children. Her mother-in-law had succeeded. Rani had lasted all of four days and by Friday had slept through her alarm, missed all her morning meetings, and been late dropping the girls off to camp.

That was when she'd realized that her mother had been getting up hours before the children to make breakfast, get herself ready for work and then be available to braid Rani's hair. And she had done it for decades, first with Rani, then Sohel, and when they were finally old enough to take care of themselves, Anaya had come along and her mother started all over again.

"Rani, is Arjun coming back here?"

Rani had talked to Arjun every day. He was getting staff lined up for the hotel but he'd asked if she wanted him to come to LA to see her.

"He's busy with the hotel."

"I'm doing a *puja* tomorrow night to thank the Lord Krishna for making your dad better. It would be nice if Arjun could come. He should see our house."

Rani looked at her mother and knew instantly what she meant. Her parents had researched Arjun and knew how wealthy he was. Rani thought about the flowered couch in the upstairs living room. The "good" couch that had been perfectly preserved underneath a plastic cover, the "new" kitchen that had been renovated fifteen years ago. There was nothing sleek, polished or grand about her parents' house. Which was exactly why she had to invite Arjun.

Arjun was well aware of her family's middle-class status but it was one thing to know it and another to see it firsthand. Plus an official event at the parents' house would take their relationship to the next level of seriousness and she wanted to see how he'd react to it.

She excused herself to go to her room and text Arjun.

Do you have plans tomorrow evening?

His response was immediate.

Yes but I could be persuaded out of them.

How about dinner and a puja at my parents' house.

Okay as long as there's dessert afterwards ;)

She smiled. It had been weeks since they'd been intimate. Surely she could find some private time for them.

Life is short. Dessert first.

She smiled as he sent back a winky face emoji with two hearts. She still couldn't believe that he loved her. When they were done texting, she booked him a room at the Beverly Wilshire. She wouldn't miss this chance to be with him.

When the next evening arrived, she decided to wear a pale pink chiffon sari with a lace trim. It was elegant and delicate. The sari had a rose-gold blouse that was skin-tight, sleeveless and cropped to a couple inches below the bra line.

She stood in front of the full-length mirror at the hotel and began getting dressed. She had purchased a pink bra with just enough support and lift to work underneath the sari blouse, as well as a matching thong. She'd blushed the whole time she was at the store, thinking of Arjun seeing her in them.

The sari also had a petticoat that started below her belly button and fell to her ankles. The main length of sari fabric was wrapped around and tucked into the petticoat to keep the sari in place. It had been a few years since Rani had worn one, and it took her a few tries to get the six yards of fabric wrapped just right.

She wore her hair loose, the way Arjun liked it. With

just five minutes to spare before he was to arrive, she quickly slid some liner around her eyes and touched her lips with gloss. She went to put on her rose-gold heels and realized that she should have tied the sari after putting on the heels to get the length right but it was too late now.

She'd just grabbed the shoes when she heard a knock on the hotel room door.

She opened the door a little breathless. And there he stood, looking even more handsome than she remembered. He was dressed in a traditional Indian kurta pajama. The long tunic top was cream-colored with maroon embroidery. The legging-like pants were the same maroon as the embroidery on the tunic. He had a matching scarf wrapped around his neck. If possible, he looked even more handsome in Indian clothes than he did in his Savile Row suits.

He put his hand on his heart as he looked at her. "Wow. You are gorgeous, Rani."

Heat slid through her as his eyes roamed over her body. She waved him in. "Sorry it's not a suite but my credit card limit is not that high."

"I couldn't care less about the room right now," he said in a thick voice. He pointed to the heels she was holding in her hand. "Let me."

She felt a wave of disappointment that he wanted to leave already. She handed him the shoes and sat down. He bent down on his knee and took her foot. *My very own Prince Charming. Hope the shoe fits.*

"I talked to Hema."

Rani leaned forward.

"She was so relieved that I'm going to break the

*rishta*," he continued. "The truth is that she's been seeing someone she has real feelings for. Now we just have to figure out a way to tell our parents."

Arjun took his time buckling the straps on the sandals, then ran his hand up Rani's leg. She shivered deliciously, craving the warmth of his body on hers. She took his hand and guided it further up her thigh.

"How much time do we have before we need to get to your parents? I don't want to be late."

She couldn't care less about being late. "We have time. I had you come early."

His face broke into a grin, his dimple sending heat racing to her core. He bent his head and kissed the inside of her thigh. Her carefully tied sari was already starting to bunch around her knees as his mouth moved upwards. She parted her legs and he gently rubbed the outside of her silky panties with his fingers, then slid them underneath the fabric and inside her. There was no hiding how she felt, just like she was sure that if she reached down and touched him, he would be hard as a rock.

He stood and hoisted her up with him. His hand was warm on her exposed lower back. He ran his fingers across her bare midriff. "Is this sari pinned?" She took out the clip that was holding the *pallu* in place. The decorated end of the sari began unraveling.

"Not anymore."

"I like a woman who knows how to tie a sari without a million pins."

The fact that he knew he'd have to undo a bunch of safety pins rankled her. Exactly how many women's saris had he taken off? Before, she hadn't let herself think about all those women because the affair was just temporary. But now? Would he be satisfied if she were the last woman he ever had?

"What's wrong?"

"Nothing."

"Rani…" He kissed her neck, then whispered across her earlobe, his breath warm and intoxicating. "I can tell when your mind has gone someplace it shouldn't." He pulled her close to him and kissed the space between her jaw and ear, and she curled her neck into his kiss, enjoying the quivers it sent down her spine.

"I was just thinking that you've had women who know how to please you in bed. Are you going to be happy with me forever? What if you stop being attracted to me?"

He took her hand and guided it down to his erection. "You feel that, Rani? You are so sexy. With most women, it takes me time to get to this point. I just have to look at you and I find it hard to control myself." He kissed the corners of her mouth. "After you, Rani, I don't want any other woman on this planet."

His words wrapped around her like a warm blanket. Never in her wildest dreams did she think she could be the one to drive a man hot with desire.

The *pallu* had already fallen to her waist, showing off the tight blouse that did nothing to hide her taut nipples. Her midriff was bare. He grabbed hold of the *pallu* and tugged. She twirled as he unwrapped the sari. He tossed the fabric on a chair.

He kissed her bare stomach and she shivered at his warm breath, her entire body responding instantly. He unbuttoned her blouse, then filled his hands with her breasts and slowly rubbed his thumbs over her nipples.

"I can't wait to see you in a Rajasthani *choli*." He murmured.

*A Rajasthani* choli. Rani stilled. A traditional outfit from his home in India. The palace he called a home.

"What's wrong?"

"You know, we haven't talked about everything that's happened. About what it all means."

Arjun cupped her face and tilted it up so he could look at her. "I was kidding about the Rajasthani *choli*. You don't have to wear it if you don't want to. I'm not going to try and control you, Rani. That's not the kind of man I am."

"It's just, there is so much to work out between us. I wasn't brought up with your wealth. My parents' house is very different than yours..."

He bent down and kissed her lightly. "I don't care if you grew up in a cardboard box on the street corner. All that matters to me is that we love each other. We're going to take it step-by-step. Let's get through tonight, then we'll sort out how to break the news to my parents."

He was oversimplifying things. But when he bent his head and claimed her mouth with heat and desire and promise, her mind went blank. She was no longer able to think about what lay ahead.

This time their lovemaking was different. It wasn't furious, despite how their desire was driven to new levels of ecstasy. They both went slower, taking the time to enjoy each other and let themselves melt into one another. Rani let herself touch and explore Arjun like he belonged to her, and the love she felt in her heart was unbearable.

Could this be real? Or was her heart was about to shatter into a million unfixable pieces?

# Sixteen

Rani had begged her mother to keep it simple. She had only been gone three hours but when she returned with Arjun, the house was chaos.

If Rani had been worried about the seventies-era decor being embarrassing, her mother had gone all out to decorate for the *puja*. Christmas lights hung around the entire living room. Midway through, her mother had run out of the white ones so multicolored bulbs were haphazardly strung on one side of the living room. A statue of Lord Krishna and his wife, Radha, was on the fireplace mantel, decorated with flowers. Tea light candles flickered at the base of the statues. The scent of incense permeated the room.

Her mother started the *puja* and everyone respect-fully bowed their heads towards the statues but Rani caught Arjun looking around her living room. While there was no judgment in his eyes, Rani wondered how his parents would feel coming to a house like hers. They lived in a literal palace.

Thankfully her mother kept the *puja* to under thirty minutes rather than her usual hour plus. When she was done, she came around with a large steel plate that contained a burning candle, red vermillion paste, and *prasad*, a sweet offering to the gods that was now blessed thanks to the *puja* and thus ready for human consumption.

Rani's mother brought the plate to the participants one by one, who put their palms over the flame to receive the light from the prayers, then dipped their fingers in the red paste and touched their foreheads. They also each took a piece of the *prasad*. When she got to Rani and Arjun, her mother waved the plate in front of their faces, then used her own finger to dot their foreheads with the red paste. "I prayed for you two, as well," she said conspiratorially. "May God bless your union and you two have a very happy life together."

Their dining room table was filled with a variety of dishes that Rani knew her mother had spent all day cooking. They sat and filled their plates.

"So, Arjun, I read an article that your mother wants a very traditional *bahu* who will help her run the household. Will you all live together in your big *bangla* in Rajasthan?" The question was asked by Rani's father.

Arjun's gaze tangled with Rani's. He cleared his throat. "Rani and I have not made any decisions. This is all so new, I think we need some time to discuss things."

Her stomach dropped. His eyes conveyed what his

mouth couldn't say. He hadn't considered the full ramifications of marrying Rani. And she hadn't, either. She was not moving to India. She'd been there a handful of times in her life and while she spoke the language and understood the culture, it didn't feel like home.

And what about his parents? While he may be able to extricate himself from his arrangement with Hema, would his parents accept her? Arjun was the most eligible bachelor in India, and by the community's standards, she was far from a prized catch.

A tense silence blanketed the room. "I think we should let Arjun eat before interrogating him," Rani's mother broke in. They switched to talking about Indian politics.

A little later, Rani caught up with her mother in the kitchen. "What are you doing? What's with the questions?"

Her mother placed her hands on her hips. "What's wrong with the questions? You think we haven't noticed that he is very evasive when we ask him about whether his family will accept you. He answers without answering. You are naive, Rani. You don't know how things work in traditional Indian families, especially *khandaani* ones like his. His parents' approval is very important and he should not be waiting too long to get it. We are just pushing him a little so he doesn't keep stringing you along."

She touched Rani's cheek. "We don't want him breaking your heart."

Rani sighed and turned away. How could she tell her mother that she hadn't thought things through? That she'd been so swept up in the moment that she had forgotten that everything her mother was saying was true? How was she supposed to tell her mother that there was a chance Arjun might not be the one walking away?

She couldn't make the same mistakes she'd made with Navin. She wasn't going to give up everything she'd worked for, and she wasn't moving to India. What remained to be seen was whether Arjun would stand up for her with his parents.

Her mother caught her arm. "Rani, we want you to be happy, above all else. Arjun seems like a decent boy, and marriage to him will leave your past behind. He cares about you. I see it by the way he looks at you, and the way he worried about your father. Did you know that he flew in the best stroke specialist in the country to see your dad?"

"What?" Rani had no idea.

"We wouldn't have found out but Anaya heard the doctors talking outside his room. We thought the hospital called Dr. McNeil but he was flown in from New York. He's a world-famous stroke specialist. Arjun got him a private jet and God knows how much he must have paid him. Doctors like that don't fly across the country for people like us."

Rani sucked in a breath. That sounded like something Arjun would do.

"No matter how rich he is, if he didn't love you, he would not have done that. And he would not have hidden it from us. He wanted your father to get better."

Her mother grabbed her hand. "I know you're afraid to go into another marriage, but you mustn't think like that. You need to consider the man you are marrying.

He is pure gold. And this time, maybe you will be more understanding with your in-laws."

Tears stung her eyes. Rani extracted her hand from her mother's grip. It always came back to her needing to make the compromises.

She didn't argue with her mother then, but she did tell Arjun she wanted to leave as soon as they could. She couldn't let her parents fall more in love with Arjun than they already were. There were some difficult conversations that she and Arjun had been avoiding. It was time to have them.

Seventeen

# Seventeen

Arjun stretched out in his seat as their plane took off towards Vegas. The night had been trying to say the least. When Rani suggested they leave, he had been happy to oblige. He hadn't fully thought through things when he had asked for Rani's hand in marriage and when he had agreed to the *puja* at her parents' house. In both instances, he'd let his love for Rani dictate what he'd done, rather than choosing the smart play. And tonight had been a good reminder of the consequences of his emotional decisions.

Rani's parents had every right to question why he hadn't told his parents about Rani. He should have called his mother the moment he returned the first time from LA but he'd decided to wait until he could fly to India and discuss it face-to-face.

There were several messages from his assistant to come back to Vegas, so he'd called for the jet immediately and Rani decided to return with him. His phone kept buzzing but he ignored it. Whatever crisis had brewed in the few hours that Arjun had been in LA could wait until the morning. Arjun was tired and wanted to enjoy a moment with Rani. Things would be hard enough for them in the next few weeks.

"Arjun, we should talk."

He nodded. "It'll be nearly midnight when we get to Vegas. Why don't you stay with me tonight? We can talk when we're both fresh in the morning."

"I don't have any of my stuff and I can't go around Vegas in this." They were still dressed in the Indian clothes they'd worn to Rani's house.

He tapped out some quick messages on his phone using the plane Wi-Fi. "I'll have someone buy some clothes for you to wear."

"At this hour?"

"It's Vegas. There are shops open 24/7."

"I meant you have people working at this late hour?"

He shrugged. "I have a personal assistant on call for things I might need." He saw the expression on her face. "What?"

"I can't even fathom this life that you have. An assistant at your beck and call to pick up clothes for your—" she paused "—for whatever I am."

He actually had several such assistants but he didn't bring that up now. He took her hand. "You are the love of my life. I know tonight was hard." He squeezed her hand. "I don't have all of the answers but I will soon.

I've been getting things lined up. I'll fly to India next weekend and talk to my parents in person."

Rani's face brightened. "Really? Do you want me to come with you?"

"Not for this trip. My parents will be furious and I don't want you to bear their wrath. Once things have settled down and they've accepted the situation, then I'll take you to meet them. Or fly them here to meet your family."

Rani frowned.

"Trust me, Rani. I need to handle my parents carefully. The news is not going to be easy on them and I have to be very strategic about how I present things. It all has to be in a certain order."

"Why?" Rani whispered.

"It's all the reasons you already know."

"I want to hear you say it. What'll be the most important thing to them?"

"Probably the fact that my mother is breaking a *vachan* to Hema's family. And it's not just the promise she made, my mother loves Hema like her own daughter and she'll be heartbroken at the idea that Hema won't be her daughter-in-law."

"How will I ever compete with that?" Rani said in a small voice.

"You won't. My mother has known Hema since she was a little girl. It's not a competition between you, just like you wouldn't try to be equal with one of my sisters. Be your own person, Rani, and in time they will come to love you just like I have."

"And what happens if they don't accept me?"

"What happens if you don't accept them?"

"What?" The question had clearly surprised Rani, but it was one of the things that had him more worried than his own parents' reaction. There were a lot of things he'd have to work out with his family, his mother especially. But Rani would also have to compromise. He couldn't move to Vegas. Most of his family holdings were in India. He was also the eldest son, which meant that he was in charge of their familial home in Rajasthan. While he could work with his mother to loosen the house rules, Rani would still have to learn to live with his parents under more restrictions than she would like.

*Will she accept the life I can give her?*

"My family is very traditional, and I'll do my best to change that but it won't happen overnight. Are you willing to be patient with me? To go into this situation knowing you might have to make some compromises?"

"Like what?" Rani said, her eyes wide and panicked.

At that moment the pilot announced that they were landing soon and due to a dust storm in Vegas, the landing would be bumpy. Rani and Arjun buckled their safety belts, each lost in his or her own thoughts.

Arjun glanced at his phone to see that his executive assistant's panic level had risen. He'd call him once they were at his condo.

A car was waiting for them when they arrived at the airport. Rani was quiet on the ride into town, no doubt contemplating the loaded question Arjun had asked her. He didn't push. When they got to his building, he used his elevator key to get them up to his condo. When they exited the elevator, his executive assistant was standing in the foyer dressed in a business suit.

Arjun groaned. While he appreciated the man's tenacity, he was in no mood to deal with whatever red tape the gaming commission had thrown his way.

"Rahul, I need a minute," he said, holding up his hand as he punched the code to get into the condo.

"No, sir, I must speak to you before you go in."

Arjun waved Rani through the open door. "Go ahead, make yourself comfortable. I'll be right in." Then he turned to Rahul, who looked like he was about to go into cardiac arrest.

"Sir, your parents are inside," he whispered.

# Eighteen

Rani had barely entered the condo when Arjun grabbed her hand. "Rani!"

"Don't bother, Arjun. We see you."

Rani turned towards the voice and recognized his mother immediately from the pictures she'd seen. Arjun's parents were not what Rani expected. Perhaps because of her experience with her mother and ex-mother-in-law, she expected a traditionally dressed woman in a sari or *salwar kameez* with the kind of jewelry that befit her status. But Jhanvi Singh was dressed in cream linen pants and a stylish light blue blouse. Her salt-and-pepper hair was stylishly cut in waves and fell around her shoulders. Her makeup was flawless even at this late hour and the only jewelry she wore were tasteful diamond solitaires. Dharampal Singh was an older version of Arjun, with nearly white hair. Tall and stately, he was dressed in a Lacoste collared shirt and khaki trousers. The couple looked like they belonged on a yacht in Monte Carlo.

Arjun moved towards his parents and bent down and touched their feet. They each placed a hand on his head. Only then did he rise and hug them. Rani knew the tradition but was surprised to see it. While touching feet was a mark of respect for elders, in modern Indian families it was only done during special occasions like marriage. Her parents, and even her ex-in-laws, didn't follow this custom on a daily basis. A deep dread spread inside her chest.

"And who is this?" his mother asked.

"This is Rani." Arjun motioned her over and Rani stepped towards them on leaden legs.

Rani joined her hands and bowed her head. "Namaste."

Arjun looked pointedly at Rani and then his parents' feet. She gave them a thin smile then bent down and did what was expected of her. They each touched her head and uttered a blessing.

"So she's the one you've been fooling around with?"

Rani froze then stepped away from them.

"Ma!"

Jhanvi's eyes blazed with anger. "We dropped everything and flew overnight from India to see if the story was true and we find you coming home in the middle of the night with her?" Then she turned to Rani. "And what good Indian girl is with a man in the middle of the night when he is not her husband?"

Rani shrank back, her mouth completely dry and

her chest so constricted she wasn't sure if she was still breathing.

"What are you talking about?" Arjun came to stand beside Rani. He touched her and she tried to focus on the warmth of his hand in the exposed dip of her lower back.

His father clicked on a tablet and turned the screen to show Arjun. "There's a story of you circulating in the media. A picture of you and Rani kissing. The story claims you're engaged."

Rani squinted to look at the headline, which blazed in red. *Hottie Arjun Getting Married to Average-Looking American Divorcée.* Right below it was a picture of them kissing. The hospital garden with its metal picnic tables was in the background. It was the day Arjun told her he loved her.

"How did this get out?" Arjun lamented.

Like that was what was important right now. Did he not see the anger in his parents' eyes?

"Someone named Anaya Gupta—I assume she's your sister—took the photo." Arjun's father looked at Rani with such anger that she felt like she'd been cut in half. She shriveled back, moving away from Arjun and towards the door as if willing it to open and let her escape. "She posted an Instagram picture saying how happy she is for her sister and used the hashtag *#IndiasHottestHottie.* That's when the story first broke. The story is all over the Indian news media. How could you be so stupid, letting people take pictures with you like that? Hema's family is furious. Her father wanted to come with us."

"What were our PR people doing? Why didn't they stop the story?" Arjun asked.

*Why is that important?* Rani shouted in her head. Why wasn't anyone addressing the real issue?

"That PR hack you hired isn't worth the dirt on my shoe." His father scoffed. "The paper called him for a comment and he was worse than useless."

"I'll fire him tomorrow."

"Already done," Dharampal responded.

*I have to get out of here or I'll scream.*

"We'll have to fix it. I'm thinking we call a press conference tomorrow morning and say the picture is being blown out of proportion. Maybe announce your engagement to Hema," his father said, all businesslike.

"How about just denying it's me in the picture. You can't see my full face."

What was Arjun saying? If they were going to be together, what good would it do lying to the media? *Unless he didn't plan on going through with the engagement after all.*

"Arjun, this story has a lot of steam in India. The only way to settle things down is to announce your engagement. Besides, Hema's family isn't willing to wait anymore."

*Say something, Arjun! Tell him that if you're announcing your engagement, it'll be to me!* Rani's tongue was superglued to the roof of her mouth. Her body trembling, she was unconsciously taking small steps towards the door behind her.

"I'm not ready to announce my engagement to Hema."

*Say the rest Arjun, say the rest*, Rani silently pleaded.

"What's not to be ready about?" Arjun's mother stepped up to him. "Your wedding is set for two months from now. Do I need to remind you what's at stake here? Hema's family has been very patient with you but you know as well as we do that if they pull out of our business partnership, you'll have to sell the Vegas hotel."

*Two months!* The wedding date was around the corner and Arjun still hadn't talked to his parents about not wanting to marry Hema? This wasn't just about him and Rani. It was about him having the courage to face his parents.

"Ma, why are we standing here talking about such important matters? You must be tired from your journey. You should rest, and we can discuss this first thing in the morning," Arjun said with maddening calm.

"I'm quite fresh," Jhanvi said. "It's early morning India time. I slept on the flight and so did your dad."

"Jhanvi, we are on India time but he's on Las Vegas time. Let him get a few hours' sleep. I'll send the jet back to get Hema. If we're going to make an announcement, she should be here with him."

Rani had never seen Arjun getting steamrolled and yet here he was, looking wearily at his parents like he wasn't going to tell them that the woman he loved was standing right there.

"Let's pick this up tomorrow morning," Arjun's father said with finality.

"What about her?" Jhanvi nodded towards Rani as if suddenly remembering she was there.

*Yes, what about me? Were you going to remember that I've been standing here this whole time or am I always going to be invisible next to your parents?*

Arjun stepped towards her and whispered quietly in her ear. "Rani, I will handle them, but not tonight. Why don't you go home? I'll have Sam take you."

Rani did not need to be told twice. She spun and Arjun had barely gotten the door open before she walked through it. She stabbed at the elevator button, silently cursing it for not lighting up. Arjun came up behind her and calmly punched a code into the keypad next to the call button.

"Rani, please understand. There is a way to deal with my parents."

"And that way is to pretend like I don't exist?"

"Believe me, this is not how I intended to introduce you to them. Right now they are only concerned about my media image. Remember, I'm the face of our hotel chain. Any scandal affects not just our family reputation but also our hotel brand and the partnership with Hema's parents' business. They're a publicly traded company and answer to shareholders. We need to deal with that situation first. If only your sister hadn't posted that picture on social media…"

*I'm not going to cry. I'm not going to beg. And I'm not going to let this be Anaya's fault.*

When the elevators dinged, Rani stepped into the carriage. "Your family image and hotel brand won't be helped by an average-looking divorcée."

He let the doors shut, and she let the tears stream down her cheeks.

# Nineteen

The next morning Arjun woke up to his mother making chai in his kitchen. He kissed her on the cheek. "I'll call the housekeeper to bring us something for breakfast."

"I'm making you *aloo paranthas* with my own hands," his mother replied in Hindi.

Arjun smiled. The thin wheat pancakes stuffed with spiced potatoes were his favorite. It was a special treat in his house to have them made by his mother.

"I've taught Hema how to make these too."

Arjun sighed as he took the cup of tea she handed him.

"Ma, I'm not going to marry Hema."

He hadn't wanted to have the conversation with his parents in front of Rani. He knew how brutally blunt his parents could be and he didn't want Rani's relationship with them affected by what they'd say in anger. But he wasn't going to let them walk all over him. This was his life and it was time to get things under control.

His mother didn't miss a beat. "Don't be stupid. Of course you are."

"I've fallen in love. I don't think it's fair to Hema to marry her when my heart belongs to someone else." He didn't want to betray Hema's confidence by telling his mother that she didn't want to marry him, either. He'd talked with Hema earlier that morning and she'd promised to come clean with her parents and tell them she didn't want to marry him. He'd explained the potential business fallout if they thought he was the only one breaking the *rishta*.

"You've been in love before," his mother said coldly. "Besides, have you forgotten the implications of breaking the *rishta* with Hema's family?"

"Our business deal benefits them too. They're astute enough to know that pulling out now is a loss for both our families."

"That's not the point and you know it. This *rishta* was a way to permanently bind our families together in a way business deals can't. And have you forgotten what a lovely girl Hema is? She knows our family *parampara*. We will never find anyone better suited to be your wife."

"Hema is a good woman but I don't love her in the way a husband should love a wife."

She fisted the dough for the *paranthas*. "Who is this girl you're in love with? The one from yesterday?"

"Yes."

"The divorcée?"

"Her name is Rani, and she's an interior architect. She's intelligent, caring and my equal in every way."

His father appeared in the kitchen doorway. "Jhanvi, you beat that dough any further and you'll break the stone counter."

"Come and listen to what your son has to say. He's fallen in love with that girl from last night, that divorcée, and he doesn't want to marry Hema." Without waiting for his father to comment she continued. "What do you see in her, Arjun? Even if you don't want to marry Hema, every eligible girl in India is dying to marry you. This girl is not particularly beautiful, she's not that thin and I saw the way she looked at you when you asked her to touch our feet. What qualities does she have that make her right for our family?"

He took a breath to keep his voice calm, doubly glad that he hadn't let Rani hear this conversation. "You're talking about the woman I love. You don't know Rani. If you did you'd see that she is beautiful inside and out. She is intelligent, accomplished, she understands me…"

"And Hema is none of those things?"

"Hema is like my sister. We've grown up together. I just don't feel for her the way I do for Rani."

"Son…" Arjun's father had been listening silently to the exchange, but the deep baritone in his voice made Arjun cringe. He recognized it. It was the voice any father used when telling his son that he was in big trouble. Arjun suddenly felt like he was ten years old and had been caught beating on his brother.

"I know what you're going to say. We made a promise to Hema's family and we always keep our *vachan*. But—"

"You don't know what I'm going to say. And since when do you interrupt your father?"

Arjun took a breath. Now was not the time to get into an argument about pointless things.

"We have been fighting to make sure that the children of our house, our daughters especially, are not corrupted by the Western influences that have taken over India. Day by day we are losing our culture. You are the eldest son. It will be your job to keep the *parampara* of the house alive after your mother and I are dead. Your wife will be the eldest *bahu* of the house and more than you, she will keep the *izzat*, the respect of our family name. She will make sure that the next generation is raised with the same values that we raised you with. Is Rani going to be able to fulfill that role?"

This was the part that worried Arjun the most. It was the argument he had avoided having with his parents his whole life, and one where there would be no winners.

"Dad, don't you think that as times have changed, we too must evolve as a family? Not to change our values, but perhaps some of our traditions, our way of doing things."

"Jhanvi and my parents arranged our marriage. We've been happily married for thirty-six years."

"But your marriage was unconventional, was it not?" Arjun's heart hammered. He knew there was no turning back if he said the next words, but he had to. "Dad, you were from a wealthy family and in those days, you married in the same money class in order to consolidate wealth. But Ma, while from a family with lineage, your family had nothing. It took a change in tradition for dad's family to accept you. And for your family to accept that I already existed, which meant you would not give birth to the household heir."

"Arjun, how dare you?" his mother said sharply.

"Even traditions have to evolve with time to stay relevant. Ma, most women of your generation were married off by the time they were sixteen. But you didn't marry my sisters off. Why are you willing to break that tradition but not others?"

"And you see where your sisters are now? They want to work, and to have their own money."

"And what's wrong with that? You know we almost lost everything ten years ago when tourism crashed in India. We all need a career to fall back on. You educated me and Sameer, so it's right to do the same for my sisters. I work, why can't Divya? In fact, for the last month she's been incredibly helpful in the Jaipur office. So many things I couldn't take care of, she has handled even better than me. What gives me and Sameer the right to run your business, Dad? Why not Divya?"

"Because that's not the way society works. One day Divya will get married and have a household with her own husband and children to look after. They won't be part of our *gharana*. Why are you suddenly questioning our way of life?"

"This must be Rani's influence," his mother muttered bitterly.

"I have always felt this way but never questioned you."

"Because we raised you the right way. A few months with that girl and look at what's happening," Jhanvi said.

Arjun sighed. He'd expected the conversation to go badly but he was drowning.

"You know nothing about Rani."

"We had her investigated when the first picture surfaced," Dharampal said.

Anger boiled inside him and the only thing keeping him calm was the realization that flying off the handle would just make things worse for him and Rani.

"She divorced her ex-husband for no apparent reason. He came from a respectable family. What makes you think she can commit to you?" Jhanvi asked.

"You have no idea what kind of guy her ex-husband is. *Khandan* isn't the only thing that determines a person's character. Rani was right to leave him. I have no doubt that she's committed to me." Even as he said the words, he shifted on his feet. The very things he loved about Rani, her independence, her strength, would clash with his everyday family life. Would she be able to adjust?

"But is she committed to our family? To our traditions?"

Arjun wanted to answer *yes*, but he couldn't. He and Rani had been avoiding the conversation because she didn't want to disappoint him, and he didn't want to face the fact that he'd have to choose between Rani and his parents. A choice that was staring him in the face now.

"She will make some compromises, and so must we," he answered carefully.

"But why?" his mother asked.

"Why what?"

"Why must we compromise our values, our ideals?"

"I'm not as traditional as you want me to be. I agree with my sisters that they should have more freedom.

Rani understands me. She can be my partner in life in a way Hema never can."

"We are not talking about this anymore. I'm making breakfast, and you will come to your senses, Arjun," his mother said decisively.

After a tensely silent breakfast, Arjun's mother excused herself. She had brought a few of her maids with her from India and the women efficiently went about cleaning the kitchen. He and his father stepped onto the balcony with a cup of chai.

"Son, I'm going to tell you about the time I married your mother."

Arjun sighed inwardly. He had heard the arranged marriage story a million times.

"Not Jhanvi, your birth mother."

Arjun looked at his father in surprise. He never talked about Arjun's birth mother. There weren't any pictures of her in the family archives, no mention of her among the older servants who knew his grandparents. The only evidence of her existence was Arjun himself.

"Your grandfather had arranged my marriage to Jhanvi when we were children. When I was barely eighteen, I fell in love with Savitri. She was beautiful and exciting, and she came from a good family who had money and status. I thought for sure my father would be happy to break the *rishta* with Jhanvi. By then her family had lost all their wealth and were no longer in the same social class as us. But my father said no. He said we made a promise to Jhanvi and her family and we didn't want their *hai*, the curse of their ill feelings."

Arjun shifted in his chair.

"But I was insistent. So much so that I ran away and

had a priest marry us without our parents present. Savitri was always traumatized by the fact that her father wasn't there to give her away. The resentment from our families ate at both of us. Despite the fact that we were married, we were never happy. And then she died giving birth to you. I think our marriage was cursed from the beginning without the blessing of our parents."

Arjun saw the sincerity in his father's eyes. While he didn't believe in curses, he could see how parental disapproval could wreak havoc on a close-knit family. There was a child inside every adult who wanted nothing more than to please his or her parents. He'd seen that longing and pain in Rani's eyes every time she talked about her parents.

"I didn't know how to care for a baby. The *aiyas* took care of you, but a servant can't provide a mother's love. My father begged forgiveness from Jhanvi's father, and I from her. She not only married me, she loved you. In fact, we delayed having children because she wanted to give you her love exclusively. I didn't love Jhanvi when we married, but I love her more now than I ever loved Savitri. She made a home for me and my children. She brought our family together. My love for her has grown with age because each day I appreciate more and more how important the things my father talked about really are. I scoffed at him when he talked about *parampara* but it's only when I didn't have it, when there was chaos in my house that I understood what he was saying. Don't make the same mistake I did."

"How are you so sure that Rani won't do for our house what Ma did? That she won't be able to bring our generations together? Maybe she is exactly what we need to bridge the divide between our *parampara* and the new world we live in. Rani grew up in a traditional household like us and she's struggled with this all her life. She understands how to handle it. She's the one who came up with the solution for Divya to work for us in the Jaipur office."

"A decision I don't agree with. I think we should have told Divya she can't work."

"And then what, Dad? Divya would meekly sit at home and be happy? She'd be miserable and fight us on every little thing, ruining the peace of the house. Instead, she's helping us run our family business and—"

"And every day she and your other sisters are feeling more emboldened to break the house rules."

"Dad, just like we modernized our hotels, we must change our household or—"

"Or all of the children will rebel like you. Arjun, have you forgotten that our wisdom stopped you from making a mistake with that other girl?"

Arjun fought the rage boiling deep in his belly. For the last ten years, he had worked tirelessly to secure and expand the family fortunes. To ensure the future for his siblings. He'd supported his parents even when he didn't agree with their decisions. He'd made a mistake with Lakshmi, but that was the inexperience of his youth. He was a thirty-eight-year-old man who managed a company worth nearly ten billion dollars.

*Does Dad still see me as that foolish boy who fell for a gold digger?*

"I'm not rebelling, Dad, I'm choosing how to live my personal life. You trust me to make critical decisions that affect our family business every day. Decisions that determine all our futures. Why can't you trust me to know what's best for me?"

"Because men cannot be trusted to differentiate between love and desire." Jhanvi's voice cut through the air. She was talking to Arjun but her gaze was fixed on her husband. She moved towards Arjun. "When you come back to India, you'll marry Hema. If you can't accept that, then I suggest you don't return."

# Twenty

"You asked to see her?" Em asked incredulously.

Rani nodded, miserably picking at the pasta salad Em had made her for lunch. They were in the kitchen of their shared apartment. Em had decorated the room in a folksy style with small pictures of chickens and ducks that had been painted by her patients. The two-person dining room table was made of reclaimed barn wood. Rani loved the cozy warmth of this kitchen. Was she really ready to go back to large, shiny appliances that only chefs knew how to use? Then she thought about making lamb *saag* and masala chai with Arjun and tears stung her eyes.

"I'm tired of everyone thinking they know best how to handle my love life. I need to meet with his mother and decide for myself whether I can be with Arjun. So I called his condo and asked if I could come over to meet with her. She said she'd been about to call and ask me over for tea. I guess great minds think alike."

"Wow." Em had a rare morning off from the hospital, and rather than sleeping or catching up on her never ending to-do list, she had spent the time keeping Rani company, listening with endless patience as she vented, then strategized, then cried about how to handle the situation.

"How much money do you think she'll offer you to remove your claws from her son?"

Rani cracked a smile. "How much should I accept?"

Em clicked on her phone, tucking her hot pink hair behind her ear. "Google says his family net worth is unknown but they're estimated to be in the top one hundred richest families in the world. I say you ask for a beach house in Hawaii."

"I jumped into things too quickly," Rani said miserably. "You should've seen him with his parents last night. They walked all over him. That's what it was like with Navin."

"And what you're like with your own parents," Em said gently.

"I've just gotten control over my life. I have the money to start my own consulting firm. I don't want to give all that up."

"You don't think true love is worth making some sacrifices?"

"That sounds great on a refrigerator magnet but you need more than love in reality. For the first time in my life, I don't have to answer to anyone but myself. I don't have to live my life because of obligations or traditions or because someone else wants to control me."

"Why does it have to be that way? You can still pursue your career dreams. As far as letting someone control your life, that's on you, Rani. You couldn't help how you grew up but you let Navin's family dominate you. I think you understand that now. This time, you're taking charge of this situation. What do you want Arjun to do?"

"I know this is wrong of me, but I want him to make the big gesture and tell me he's going to give it all up. I need to know that he's willing to sacrifice for me. I'm not getting into another one-way marriage."

When she arrived at Arjun's condo, she was immediately struck by the change. The furnishings were the same, all his stuff was in the same place, but the air was literally different. The kitchen was fragrant with the smell of cardamom and cinnamon. A gray-haired woman in a navy sari Rani didn't recognize let her in and asked her to sit on the couch, then disappeared. As she looked over at the kitchen, two different women dressed in the same navy saris were moving about, preparing trays. Rani sat uncomfortably on the couch. Even the stunning view didn't soothe the churning in her stomach.

"Ah Rani, you're here." Arjun's mother was dressed in dark silk pants and a rich green tunic with gold embroidery. Her salt-and-pepper hair was pulled back into a bun, and elegantly simple emerald solitaires glittered at her ears. By comparison, after some panicked wardrobe flinging, Em had helped Rani pair one of her suit pants with a cream-colored silk button-down blouse.

Her jewelry was a single pearl on a gold chain and small pearl earrings.

Rani's mouth was dry as she stood. She suddenly realized she didn't know how to address Arjun's mother. Mrs. Singh seemed too impersonal and Auntie seemed too casual. She managed a namaste.

Jhanvi nodded toward the couch. "Sit. What will you have? Chai or coffee?"

Rani didn't want anything but she smiled politely. "Whatever you're having."

Jhanvi clicked her fingers and yet another navy sari-clad woman appeared. "Gauri, chai." The woman vanished.

"Thank you for seeing me. I appreciate the opportunity to clear the air." Rani delivered her practiced opening with a throat so tight that her voice came out in a croak.

Jhanvi gave her a tight-lipped smile. "When a son gets taken in by a woman, it's a mother's job to get to know her."

Rani's stomach knotted even tighter. Two women appeared carrying trays. One contained a tea service and another an assortment of sandwiches, cookies and Indian sweets.

Rani took a sip of the perfectly brewed masala chai that was handed to her, then set the cup on the table. "What would you like to know about me?"

Jhanvi took several slow sips of her tea before setting her cup down. She picked up a small plate filled with cucumber sandwiches and held it out to Rani, who shook her head. "Try them. My cook, Neelu, makes these with fresh cilantro chutney."

Rani selected one and set it on her plate.

Jhanvi took a delicate bite of her sandwich and Rani tried not to fidget.

"So, what are your plans after you marry my son?"

"Arjun hasn't asked me to marry him." Rani immediately regretted the glib words. She knew what Jhanvi's response would be before the woman even spoke.

"I think you know that we would not be meeting if my son wasn't serious about you, so let's talk frankly."

Rani nodded contritely. She felt like she was a teenager who'd been caught with a boy in her bed.

"What specific plans are you interested in?"

"Let's start with when you plan to move to India."

*So much for easing into the conversation with a simple question.* "Arjun and I haven't discussed where we will live, but I'm sure we can work something out."

Jhanvi leaned forward. "Our home, Arjun's home, is in India. Do you think he'll be happy living in America?"

*No, he won't.* "The hotel in Vegas will need oversight, and as Arjun expands the business globally, we will have to be flexible with where we're based," Rani said evenly.

"That sounds ideal in theory but it's not practical. You are both quite old now and will want to have children soon. You can't take children from house to house. They will need a home and that home will be the one where Arjun, and his father, grew up. Our *khandani haveli.* The family palace."

Rani bit her tongue to keep from saying something she'd regret. She and Arjun had talked about the fact that they both wanted children. Although Rani was loath to admit it, she knew Jhanvi was correct in pointing out that children needed a home base. But settling the details of her future with Arjun was not the point of this conversation with his mother.

"These are all important decisions that Arjun and I will make," she said with a teary smile.

"But these decisions are not just for you and Arjun to make."

*And there it is.* What she had come to find out. Rani tilted her head and looked at Jhanvi.

"I understand you grew up in a respectable Indian household, so surely you know these are family decisions, and ones that cannot be taken lightly given how many lives this affects."

Rani bristled at the way Jhanvi said "respectable" as though she meant to put air quotes around the word.

"I understand completely. And while I *respect* the traditions and customs of your house, I think there are some things that a husband and wife must decide together. Surely you and Arjun's dad make many such decisions."

Jhanvi visibly bristled. "You aren't comparing this… this relationship you have with my son to the thirty-six years of marriage that my husband and I share? And we are the eldest generation in our house. When my in-laws were living, we bent to their every wish."

"And how did that make you feel as a daughter-in-law? Did you love your in-laws?" Rani knew she was really pushing the boundaries of appropriateness but she wanted to find some common ground with Jhanvi.

Jhanvi smiled. "I won't insult your intelligence by claiming that I loved my in-laws like a daughter would have. At first I resented and tolerated them, but as my children grew, I came to respect them and understand why they did things the way they did."

It was as honest an answer as Rani would ever get and hope bloomed in her chest. "But there are things you did differently. For example, educating your daughters."

Jhanvi reached across the couch to pat Rani's hand. "Rani, why don't we talk about what's really bothering both of us and stop circling around the real issues. I wanted to talk to you to see whether you're willing to make the sacrifices it will take to be a part of Arjun's life, and you asked to meet me to see just how tyrannical I'll be as a mother-in-law."

Rani smiled at Jhanvi, her directness reminding her so much of Arjun that she couldn't help but like the woman.

"Then how about I lay my cards on the table. I was married into a family where the parents controlled everything—the money, what we did, what we ate, who we were friends with. It was suffocating and I want to know if that's what your household is like."

Jhanvi took another cucumber sandwich; Rani hadn't touched hers. "And that is exactly why we are concerned about you, dear. We ran a background check on you and know that per your divorce decree, you parted because of irreconcilable differences. There was no mention of abuse or infidelity. Controlling in-laws are hardly a reason to leave your husband."

Rani took a breath. "It depends on one's perspective, and my situation was more complex than that. But it is also the reason that I hope we can come to an understanding about how we will interact. It's not a conversation I had before my prior marriage."

Jhanvi set down her plate. "Well, to answer your question, Dharampal and I are involved in all of the big life decisions. Arjun is in charge of the household finances and I don't care what he spends his money on or whether his wife tells the cook to make chicken tikka for dinner or *daal makhani*." She paused, as if trying to decide how to say the next part. "But we will have a role in determining who he will marry and his wife will follow the same house rules as my daughters. No late evenings without Arjun, and respectable friends. I don't want my *bahu* to work outside the house unless it's with Arjun like Divya is doing. We are a close family and are very involved in each other's lives."

Rani's mouth soured. "What if I disagree with your rules?" Rani hadn't meant to make it sound like a question and kicked herself for not being more forceful.

Jhanvi smiled. "I asked you before where you planned to live as a test question. There is no choice in that matter. Arjun will never live anywhere other than India. The fact that you think you have a choice tells me that you either don't know my son very well or you are living in a fantasy bubble that is about to burst. So I ask you to consider how much you're willing to give up for my son."

"I realize compromises need to be made, but why must I do all the sacrificing?"

"Ah, the optimism of youth." She took a bite of her sandwich. "Rani, dear, even in progressive societies like America, women talk about how they are responsible for too much of the domestic duties. More women leave their jobs when they have children than men."

"There are practical reasons why more women take

time off to care for infants. They have to recover from childbirth and men can't breastfeed."

"Exactly, Rani. Arjun is responsible for not just his financial future but that of his siblings too. He's not going to become a stay-at-home dad, as you Americans say. So what type of life are you picturing together? Exactly what are you expecting he will give up for you? What are you willing to give up for him?"

"I love Arjun and I'm willing to give up the world for him." She paused, trying to find the right words. "But I expect equality in our marriage. And the big decisions about our life will be between me and him."

"Well, then you truly do not understand my son."

Rani stood, done with diplomacy. "I think we've both gotten what we wanted out of this conversation."

Jhanvi stood and smiled.

Rani thanked her for the meeting. Now she had to face Arjun.

# Twenty-One

Arjun paced his office. Rani and his mother were meeting less than a mile away. *Should I go check on her?* He knew what his mother could be like. Yet he couldn't go. Rani had insisted that she wanted to meet with his mother alone and promised she would come see him afterwards. It was just as well; he wouldn't always be around to mediate disagreements between Rani and his parents and Rani had to make the decision about what she could handle.

*She's strong. She stood up to me. She can do this.*

He looked at his watch again. Only two minutes had passed since the last time he'd checked.

A knock on his door startled him. He had asked his assistant to bring Rani to his office as soon as she was done with his mother. He looked up to see her looking breathtakingly beautiful, and weary, like she'd been beaten down for hours.

He pulled her into his arms, not caring about the glass walls or prying eyes. Her body melted against his.

"That bad, huh?"

She pushed against his chest and lifted her face. "It wasn't bad. It was clarifying."

Acid churned in his stomach. "What do you mean?"

"Arjun, what are we thinking? How is this ever going to work? Every day will be a battle between me and your parents. I've done that before, and I can't. Not again. I don't want to give up my career to move to India and play housewife."

"You don't have to give up your career. You can open up your own design firm. My hotels alone have enough business to keep you busy for years."

She stepped back from him. "You don't get it. I don't want to be dependent on you. I want my freedom. I want to be able to work late if I need to, go out with friends at night if I want to. I don't want to fight over the simplest requests. I've lived that way all my life and I won't do it anymore."

"I'm not going to lie to you. My parents will always be a big part of my life. But we can work it out. As you Americans say, I come with baggage."

Her face crumpled. "You mother made it sound like I'd have no control over my life."

"I haven't asked you to give up a single thing, Rani."

"Okay, then tell me how it'll work between us?"

He blew out a breath, his chest so tight that he had trouble getting it all out. It was a conversation they should have had a while ago. A talk that he had avoided because he didn't like going into a meeting without having the answers.

"You can open your own design firm and we can live part time here and part time in India. If you don't want my business, that's fine. I'm not saying it'll be easy but we'll work on getting my parents to loosen the rules. If we live here part time, it won't be as bad."

"And what happens when we have children? We drag them with us on your private plane every time I get tired of living in India? Would you be happy having them grow up in a hotel?"

"We don't have to figure everything out right now. It'll be years before we have children."

"I'm thirty-six, Arjun. If we want children, there aren't a lot of years that we can wait."

Why was she being so stubborn? He was trying to meet her halfway and she was coming up with all the reasons why it wouldn't work rather than helping him find solutions like she usually did.

"I know your heart is in the right place and you want to make it work just as desperately as I do. But I think your mother has actually thought things through more than we have."

He clasped her hands. "I don't have it all worked out, but can you give me a chance to find a way?"

Her eyes were shining and the desperate look she gave him cut through his heart like a knife. He kissed her softly. "Give me some time to come up with a plan. Can you do that?"

She wrapped her arms around his neck and kissed him fiercely, her body pressed close to his, her mouth hungry on his, her fingers grasping his hair. When she released him, her face was wet. She turned and walked out, and he was left with a hole in the pit of his stomach.

*Why did that feel like a goodbye kiss?*

# Twenty-Two

Arjun was drained. He stood at his kitchen stove watching the tea boil and looked at his watch. Rani had asked to come over and he was looking forward to holding her in his arms.

His parents had just left after a volatile two days. Hema had found the courage to tell her parents she didn't want to marry him but her parents had reacted the same way as his. They felt that Hema didn't know what was best for her and was making a rash decision. They'd called Jhanvi and Dharampal to reiterate that they'd given their daughter an ultimatum: to marry Arjun or be disowned. They had also expressed anger at Arjun for his indiscretions with Rani. Meanwhile, the media storm hadn't let up.

The only win for Arjun was that he'd prevented his

parents from making an announcement about him and Hema. He'd told them in no uncertain terms that he would only marry Rani. Their response was that he wasn't welcome back into the family home if he didn't marry Hema. After her conversation with Rani, his mother was convinced that Rani would add fuel to the discord that already existed with his sisters, especially Divya.

As soon as the security guard downstairs alerted him that Rani had arrived, he took the tea off the stove and went to wait by the elevators. When the doors opened, his breath caught. Rani was wearing jeans and a V-neck shirt that showed off her curves beautifully. She smiled at him and he pulled her into his arms, savoring the feel of her against his body. He let her warm vanilla smell soothe the storm raging inside him.

*She's the woman I love. How can I spend my life with someone else, knowing she exists?*

He led her to the kitchen. "I didn't have time to make a full meal, but I made you some masala chai." She smiled and perched on the island stool while he poured the tea into two cups.

"It was rough with your parents."

He nodded. "They need some time." He tried—and failed—to sound convincing for her. "It'll be better once the media coverage dies down."

She shook her head. "You and I both know it's about more than bad publicity. I'm all wrong for your family."

His stomach clenched. He wanted to reassure her but his words would just sound hollow.

She reached out and grabbed his hands and he wove his fingers through hers.

"Arjun, I've been doing a lot of thinking. I've never loved anyone like I love you. And that's why I'm going to let you go." Her voice cracked.

His heart squeezed painfully in his chest. "You're going to have to explain that one to me."

She smiled sadly at him. "Have you looked at yourself in the mirror? You look horrible."

"Thanks so much. I haven't had time to get a facial," he joked.

"The stress is killing you and it's only been a few days." She looked down. "Think about how you're feeling right now. Can you imagine life like this every day? Constantly having to choose between me and your parents? This kind of burden will kill you, and I love you too much to do that to you. It was foolish for us to think that there was a magical way we could make it all work."

"So you want to give up? Throw it all away? Do you know how special it is to have what we have? To feel the way we do about each other?"

"Yes I do! But I also know what it's like to be trapped and feel like there's no escape. That's how it would be in your house. All my life, I've had no control over my own destiny. I did what my parents asked, and then I lived the way that my ex in-laws wanted. I can't do it anymore. I won't be the obedient *bahu* your mother is looking for, and it's going to create strife in your family. I'll be yet another burden on you and I don't want to become yet another person you have to manage in your life like you do with your sisters and brother."

Tears rolled down her cheeks. *She is unyielding*, his mother had said. He wanted to pull Rani close but she pulled her hands away from him and he let her. For the first time in his life, he felt beaten. He didn't want Rani to feel like a life with him would be the kind of prison she'd endured with her ex, yet he didn't have anything different to offer her. He'd been hoping that together they could come up with a middle ground where both their needs could be met.

"I wish more than anything that I'd never married Navin. That I didn't have the scars that are stopping me from believing that we can somehow make this work."

He wanted to beg her, plead with her to rethink what she was saying. Convince her that things would be different. But the words stuck in his mouth. She needed him to give up everything for her. His family, his business, his life.

When she kissed him on the cheek and left, he didn't stop her.

# Twenty-Three

How was it that the very person she went out of her way to avoid always ended up right in her path? Rani smiled as she passed Arjun in the hall. He gave her a clipped smile back then strode by. There were no more dimpled smiles for her.

She felt ravaged inside. The Mahal hotel was two days away from opening and for the last few weeks, she'd been onsite every day to make sure the finishing touches were done right. Arjun had moved his offices to the hotel and himself into the owners condo. Her heart squeezed painfully every time she thought of him sleeping in the four-poster bed where they'd made love for the first time.

She turned back to see him walking away. They had

survived a month and a half of pretending they were just work colleagues. What was two more days?

After the opening, she was officially done at RKS. When Arjun had insisted she remain in charge, there had been some grumblings from Delia, which Rani calmed by announcing that she planned to leave at the end of the contract. That seemed to placate everyone. She had made it very clear to Ian Rabat that if he tried to tarnish her reputation like he had Bob's, Rani would do the same to him. She felt fairly confident that her break from RKS would be amicable.

In the last month, five different firms had given her amazing employment offers. Arjun's hotel had already been featured in several travel magazines and each piece had commented on the unique interior design of the hotel. It was fully booked for its first three months.

Rani had rejected all of the job offers. Instead, she had channeled the endless hours of sleepless nights into setting up her own interior architecture firm. She'd sunk every penny she had into buying basic computer equipment and software. She couldn't afford office space or staff until she got her first contract but things were looking promising on that front. She had already signed a small restaurant in Vegas and had meetings lined up with several other businesses. Nothing as big as Arjun's hotel, but she didn't have the team for something like that. She'd start off small and as she built her business, she could take on bigger projects.

Her career was finally taking off, but she couldn't find the joy in everything going well for her. It was as though there was a deep worm burrowing through her soul and emptying the happiness out of her. She felt like a shell with nothing left inside. Every cell in her body craved Arjun, longed and ached for him. *It'll get better with time*, Rani kept telling herself. Except each day she became hollower inside.

Her cell phone buzzed. It was a text from Anaya. Heads up! Amma saw this. Rani clicked on the link in the text. It was an article in a popular Indian magazine. After she scrolled past the ads, the headline stopped her heart. *Arjun and Hema, India's Hottest Couple, to Tie the Knot in a Month.* She had never seen a picture of Hema but there she was with Arjun's family. She stood tall by his side, classically beautiful in a Rajasthani *lehngah*, a red skirt adorned with mirrored jewels and a matching cropped top choli that left her stomach exposed. She had one hand on Arjun's arm and the other holding Jhanvi's hand. A perfect family.

Rani's phone rang. It was her mother. She hadn't told her parents about the breakup with Arjun but it was time to face the music.

"That rascal. How could he cheat you like this?" Her mother spared no niceties as she cursed out Arjun. Rani let her mother vent her frustrations.

"*Amma*, we broke up a month ago."

The line went silent and Rani's heart lurched. She had avoided telling her parents because she didn't want to lose them and Arjun all at the same time. She should've been nervous, afraid of what her mother would say, but she found herself not giving a damn. It was like she was going through the motions of life but not feeling anything.

"What happened, Rani?" her mother asked quietly.

"I met his parents and it was clear they would never accept me. Arjun was ready to go against them but I didn't want him to. I didn't want to make the same mistake I made with Navin. I would go into that house and be unhappy."

"Are you happy now without him?"

"No." Tears streamed down her face. It seemed to be the only thing she could do: cry until the tears dried up and then curl up on her bed and wait until she had fresh tears.

"Then what is the point of your stubbornness?"

Rani closed her eyes. "It's not stubbornness. It's self-preservation. I don't want to end up the way I did after Navin."

"So are you feeling better now than you did back then?"

The question gave Rani pause. She was in a better place. She had her career, she had future plans. And yet she'd never felt emptier in her life.

"I didn't mourn losing Navin. I mourned losing you and Dad. I need you to get through this. I don't want to lose you again, *Amma*."

"You won't, Rani. We were wrong in the way we treated you, I see that now. If something had happened to your father and you weren't here—" Her voice broke. "You are our daughter and we should have shared in your pain, not pushed you away."

Rani hung up with her mother and stared at Arjun's

wedding announcement. She tried to picture herself where Hema stood. The article called Hema beautiful and elegant. Rani would always be the average-looking divorcée.

*9>He likes the finer things in life. And he should have them.*

# Twenty-Four

It should have been one of the proudest moments of Arjun's life, but all he felt was restless. His hotel's grand opening was perfect. Nothing was out of place. Normally hotels did a soft opening to work out the kinks, but they hadn't had the time. It was a huge risk, but he'd spent every waking minute making sure they were ready. Not that he'd been able to sleep much anyway.

He glanced at the four-poster bed where he and Rani had made love for the first time. When he'd moved into the owners condos, he had taken one of the other bedrooms, unable to face the memories of his first night with Rani.

But then he'd walked into the master bedroom in the middle of the night and slept there. The linens had been changed but he could still smell and feel Rani in the bed.

His phone buzzed, reminding him it was time to go downstairs. The opening night party was tonight and his parents and siblings were waiting for him. He silenced the buzzer. He could be late.

He ran his hands over the luxurious bedding and closed his eyes. He could see her sitting on the bed, telling him how handsome he looked and fretting about her own clothes for the evening. They would discuss who they had to talk to at the party tonight and how to make sure that his brother, Sameer, didn't end up in the tabloids tomorrow. If he kept his eyes closed, he could almost see the life he could've had with her.

A knock on the door forced him to get back to the real world.

"Dude, you're five minutes late. Ma sent me up here to make sure you weren't dead." Sameer greeted him at the door with an easy smile. Like Arjun, he was dressed in a classic black tuxedo, except his white bow tie was a little crooked and his hair looked like he'd just gotten out of bed. Normally Arjun would have said something, but what did it matter?

"Hey, you okay, bro?"

Arjun nodded, then patted his brother on the shoulder. "Do you mind asking Ma and Dad to come up here? I need to discuss something with them."

Sameer rolled his eyes, then disappeared. It wasn't unusual for Arjun to meet with his parents before a major event.

Arjun ran his hands over the wood carving on the door. Diwali was his favorite holiday. The return of the Lord Rama, whose wife had followed him into a fourteen-year banishment. Would Rani follow him? He had heard through his staff that she was leaving RKS and that she was starting her own firm. He felt a surge of pride for her. She'd been right to end things between them. She could achieve so much more without his obligations weighing her down.

He left the door ajar for his parents, who arrived a few minutes later. His father wore a tuxedo and his mother glittered in a black sari with Swarovski crystals on the *pallu*. They looked at him expectantly.

He handed his laptop to his father, who gave him a puzzled look.

"That holds the proverbial keys to the hotel, and to our entire empire. I organized all the files so you can easily access anything you need."

"I don't understand," his father said, sounding bewildered.

"I'm not marrying Hema. I don't know why you issued a press release with that old picture of all of us together. I've been very clear about my intentions. You gave me an ultimatum that I either marry Hema or leave the family. So I'm giving you back your empire."

"Arjun!" His mother sounded shocked.

"After tonight, you won't see me again."

His parents looked dumbstruck.

"*Beta*, what nonsense is this?" His father's voice was louder now.

"You can't be serious," his mother exclaimed. "Is this about Rani?"

"This is about me. And my life. I don't want to be bullied into who I marry or how I live my life. I love you both, and not being a part of this family will kill me.

But if you're willing to lose me over your stubbornness, then I'm your son, and no less firm in my convictions."

Jhanvi sat on the chaise longue in the sitting area. "You're willing to give up everything for that girl."

"Don't you see? I love Rani precisely because of who she is, the way she thinks. I never wanted her to yield to you or follow our family *parampara*. I wanted her to help me change your way of thinking to be more like hers."

"Why are you speaking in past tense?"

"Because I took too long to come to the realization that she was not the one who needed to change. I was."

Rani sat at the bar, nursing a cup of coffee. She would've left the opening night party hours ago but it turned out that several of the potential clients she'd been courting were here. In fact, most of the who's who of Vegas were here. She'd already set up two more pitch meetings.

She stared into the coffee cup, trying to find happiness in how far she'd come in the six short months since she'd first met Arjun. She'd gone from being a junior architect to starting her own company. But all she could think about was how she wished she could tell Arjun that the coffee was too bitter and he needed to find a new vendor, that his hotel was awesome, and that she was finding it really hard to give a damn about the career she cared so much about. More than anything, she wanted to tell him that she'd follow him anywhere he wanted to take her. So what if they moved to India and she had to endure his stifling household? She'd get to hold him every night. She had all the control she wanted and yet she couldn't get the one thing she needed.

"Rani, dear, do you mind if I sit here?"

Rani couldn't have been more surprised to see Arjun's mother take a seat next to her. She had seen Arjun's entire family from far away, taking the requisite publicity shots at the ribbon cutting earlier. But what could Jhanvi possibly want with her now that Arjun and Hema were getting married?

Jhanvi didn't wait for permission as she perched herself on the bar stool, and Rani couldn't help but admire the elegant way in which she managed the feat in a sari. Rani herself had dressed for the occasion in a floor-length royal-blue gown with a low back and a slit in the side.

Arjun's mother ordered a whiskey on the rocks. Her drink was delivered immediately.

"You look beautiful, dear. That color really suits you."

"Thank you."

"I noticed you earlier at the ribbon cutting so I told the security people to find you."

"You were looking for me?" She had not expected that. Surely the woman was too busy planning Arjun's big fat Indian wedding to worry about Rani.

She ignored Rani's question. "Do you know that I became a mother before I was a wife?" Rani sensed the question was rhetorical and kept her eyes on Jhanvi, giving the woman her undivided attention.

"The first time I held Arjun, he looked into my eyes with such innocent love, and I knew in that moment, even though I hadn't given birth to him, he was my son. I agreed to marry his father not because I loved Dharampal but because I'd fallen in love with Arjun. Among all my children, Arjun holds a special part of my heart. I always want to protect him." She gestured around her. "All this seems to attract the wrong sort towards him."

What was she saying? "I was never interested in Arjun's wealth…"

"You misunderstand me. I've been shielding him from having his heart broken for years. His father once broke my heart and I didn't want Arjun to go through that. But it seems that's exactly what I've done."

Her chest tightened. "What're you saying?"

"I'm saying it's clear that my son is in love with you and that he's willing to give up everything for you."

Rani's heart jumped into her throat and she sat straighter. "What do you mean he's willing to give up everything for me?"

"We gave him an ultimatum that if he didn't marry Hema, he would be disowned. So tonight, he left the family."

Rani gasped. *He did that for me?* Why hadn't he told her what he was planning to do?

"We wanted to scare him. Not in a million years did I think he would actually leave the family. So I've come to beg you to bring him back to us." Jhanvi's voice cracked.

Rani looked at her shining eyes and suddenly realized that the two of them shared something very powerful. A love for Arjun. And that made her feel a little closer to Jhanvi.

She reached out and grabbed Jhanvi's hand. "It was

never my intention for him to leave the family. I just wanted him to stand up to you."

The big gesture she'd been waiting for was not for him to forsake everything he held dear. Then it hit her. Just like she'd been waiting for Arjun to make the big gesture, he had been waiting for her to tell him that she was strong enough to deal with what might come their way. He'd been waiting for her big gesture.

Rani looked into Jhanvi's eyes, and the jumble of thoughts and emotions that had haunted her for the last weeks tumbled into place. A sudden clarity swept through her. "We can find a way to share him, can't we?" She squeezed Jhanvi's hand.

A tear dropped onto Jhanvi's cheek and she wiped it away, smearing her makeup. She clutched Rani's hand and nodded.

She drank her whiskey in one gulp, then got down from the stool abruptly. Rani looked at her questioningly. "A mother should know when to not interfere," she said with a smile. Rani turned to see Arjun standing there. He was dressed in jeans and a T-shirt, looking like the man who lit her heart on fire from the first time she'd seen him.

He raised a brow at his mother, who motioned to the seat she'd just vacated then blew him a kiss and walked away.

"Ms. Gupta, do you mind if I sit?"

She smiled. "I don't know. It might cost you a billion dollars."

He grinned at her and she nearly fainted at the sight of his dimple. "It's worth the price."

He shooed the attentive bartender away. "I'm sorry it

took me so long to realize what you were saying. I love you for who you are, and I was asking you to change that when what I should've been doing is showing you that I'll be there for you. Can I beg for your forgiveness? Am I too late to convince you to love a poor man with no home, no family and not a penny to his name?"

She smiled. "I see your new status as an improvement. Though I don't think it'll last too long." Rani turned to point at his mother, who had moved away but was hovering in the distance.

"You weren't the only one who handled it wrong," Rani continued. "I shouldn't have put everything on you and your parents. It's my life and I need to be the one strong enough to dictate the terms. And I am. All I need to know is that you'll be by my side."

He let out an audible sigh. "If there's anything I've learned in the last month, it's that I can't breathe without you, Rani."

She sighed. "This is how it'll work. My company is mine to run as I see fit. You will not interfere. We live here in Vegas part time, and I'm going to design a small house for us on your family property in Rajasthan. We'll live there the rest of the time. On your land but not under the same roof as your parents. We will raise our children there. Speaking of which, we will have no less than two but no more than three children. I get to name the girls and you get to name the boys, but I have veto power over names that sound dumb."

He grinned. "You forgot one thing?"

"What?"

He got up from the stool, then fell on one knee in front of her.

She gasped.

"Rani Gupta, I've loved you since the first moment we met. You make me whole. I want us to write the next chapters of our life together, to create our happy ending. Will you marry me?"

Her heart burst with love for him.

He pulled out a ring with a round solitaire. It was simple and elegant and just right for her.

"Yes, Arjun, I will." He stood and wrapped his arms around her. The telltale flashes of cameras clicked nearby but neither of them cared.

"I do believe you designed a tacky wedding chapel in this hotel, didn't you?"

She laughed. "Don't you dare call my designs tacky! It's actually a very tasteful chapel, complete with a traditional Hindu wedding *mandap*."

"Then what do you say we do this Vegas-style and spend the night as husband and wife?"

*10>Once he gets what he wants, he doesn't let go.*

\* \* \* \* \*

*If you love Arjun and Rani,*
*you won't want to miss*
*Divya's story*
*by Sophia Singh Sasson*
*coming in*
*February 2021*
*exclusively from*
*Harlequin Desire!*

# COMING NEXT MONTH FROM

# DESIRE

## Available September 1, 2020

### #2755 TRUST FUND FIANCÉ

*Texas Cattleman's Club: Rags to Riches* • by Naima Simone
When family friend Reagan Sinclair needs a fake fiancé to access her trust fund, businessman Ezekiel Holloway is all in—even when they end up saying "I do"! But this rebellious socialite may tempt him to turn their schemes into something all too real...

### #2756 RECKLESS ENVY

*Dynasties: Seven Sins* • by Joss Wood
Successful CEO Matt Velez never makes the first move...until the woman who got away, Emily Arnott, announces her engagement to his nemesis. Jealousy pushes him closer to her than he's ever been to anyone. Now is it more than envy that fuels his desire?

### #2757 ONE WILD TEXAS NIGHT

*Return of the Texas Heirs* • by Sara Orwig
When a wildfire rages across her property, Claire Blake takes refuge with rancher Jake Reed—despite their families' decades-long feud. Now one hot night follows another. But will the truth behind the feud threaten their star-crossed romance?

### #2758 ONCE FORBIDDEN, TWICE TEMPTED

*The Sterling Wives* • by Karen Booth
Her ex's best friend, Grant Singleton, has always been off-limits, but now Tara Sterling has inherited a stake in his business and must work by his side. Soon, tension becomes attraction...and things escalate fast. But can she forgive the secrets he's been keeping?

### #2759 SECRET CRUSH SEDUCTION

*The Heirs of Hansol* • by Jayci Lee
Tired of her spoiled heiress reputation, designer Adelaide Song organizes a charity fashion show with the help of her brother's best friend, PR whiz Michael Reynolds. When her long-simmering crush ignites into a secret relationship, will family pressure—and Michael's secret—threaten everything?

### #2760 THE REBEL'S REDEMPTION

*Bad Billionaires* • by Kira Sinclair
Billionaire Anderson Stone doesn't deserve Piper Blackburn, especially after serving time in prison for protecting her. But now he's back, still wanting the woman he can't have. Could her faith in him lead to redemption and a chance at love? _____

*Billionaire Anderson Stone doesn't deserve
Piper Blackburn, especially after serving time in prison.
But now he's back, still wanting the woman he can't
have. Could her faith in him lead to redemption
and a chance at love?*

*Read on for a sneak peek at*
The Rebel's Redemption *by Kira Sinclair*

He had no idea what he was doing. But that didn't matter. The millisecond the warmth of her mouth touched his, nothing else mattered.

Like it ever could.

The flat of his palm slapped against the door beside her head. Piper's leg wrapped high across his hip. Her fingers gripped his shoulders, pulling her body tighter against him.

He'd never wanted to devour anything or anyone as much as he wanted Piper.

Her lips parted beneath his, giving him the access he desperately craved. The taste of her, sweet with a dark hint of coffee, flashed through him. And he wanted more.

One taste would never be enough.

That thought was clear, even as everything else in the world faded to nothing. Stone didn't care where they were. Who was close. Or what was going on around them. All that mattered was Piper and the way she was melting against him.

His fingers tangled in her hair. Stone tilted her head so he could get more of her. Their tongues tangled together in a dance that was years late. Her nails curled into his skin, digging in and leaving stinging half-moons. But her tiny breathy pants made the bite insignificant.

He needed more of her.

Reaching between them, Stone began to pop the buttons on her blouse. One, two, three. The backs of his fingers brushed against her silky, soft skin, driving the need inside him higher.

Pulling back, Stone wanted to see her. He'd been fantasizing about this moment for so long. He didn't want to miss a single second of it.

Piper's head dropped back against the wall. She watched him, her gaze pulsing with the same heat burning him from the inside out.

But instead of letting him finish the buttons, her hand curled around his, stopping him.

The tip of her pink tongue swept across her parted lips, plump and swollen from the force of their kiss. Moisture glistened. He leaned forward to swipe his own tongue across her mouth, to taste her once more.

But her softly whispered words stopped him. "Let me go."

Immediately, Stone dropped his hands and took several steps away.

Conflicting needs churned inside him. No part of him would consider pushing when she'd been clear that she didn't want his touch. But the pink flush of passion across her skin and the glitter of need in her eyes… He felt the same echo throbbing deep inside.

"I'm sorry."

"You seem to be saying that a lot, Stone," she murmured.

"I shouldn't have done that." He felt the need to say the words, even though they felt wrong. Everything inside him was screaming that he should have kissed her. Should have done it a hell of a long time ago.

Touching her, tasting her, wanting her was right. The most right thing he'd ever done.

But it wasn't.

Piper deserved so much more than he could ever give her.

*Don't miss what happens next in…*
The Rebel's Redemption *by Kira Sinclair.*
*Available September 2020 wherever*
*Harlequin Desire books and ebooks are sold.*

Harlequin.com

# IF YOU ENJOYED THIS BOOK
# WE THINK YOU WILL ALSO LOVE

## HARLEQUIN
# PRESENTS

*Escape to exotic locations where passion knows no bounds.*

Welcome to the glamorous lives of royals and billionaires, where passion knows no bounds. Be swept into a world of luxury, wealth and exotic locations.

**8 NEW BOOKS AVAILABLE EVERY MONTH!**